THE GIRL IN THE MIRROR

A Novel in Poems and Journal Entries

MEG KEARNEY

A Karen & Michael Braziller Book

PERSEA BOOKS / NEW YORK

For Elizabeth Ann Smith

(1938–1983)

Persea Books, Inc.
277 Broadway, Suite 708
New York, NY 10007

Library of Congress Cataloging-in-Publication Data

Kearney, Meg.
The girl in the mirror : a novel in poems and journal entries / Meg Kearney.—
1st ed.
     p. cm.
"A Karen and Michael Braziller Book."
Sequel to: The secret of me.
Summary: In a series of poems and journal entries, seventeen-year-old Lizzie grieves over the death of her adoptive father, as her plans for college and search for her birth mother are put on hold. Includes a guide to poetic forms.
Includes bibliographical references (p.).
ISBN 978-0-89255-385-3 (trade pbk. : alk. paper)
[1. Novels in verse. 2. Adoption–Fiction. 3. Grief—Fiction.] I. Title.
PZ7.5.K43Gi 2012
[Fic]—dc23

                    2011045052

Designed by Rita Lascaro
Manufactured in the United Sates of America
First Edition

"[Lizzie's] father, whose heart was a cause for concern in *The Secret of Me*, has died shortly before the novel opens and Lizzie is devastated. We sense the terror this child has of losing parents because her sense of loss of her birth parents is still a profound stone around her neck. Lizzie plummets into a nightmare world...surviving by writing poems and journaling so vividly that she brings us right along with her.... Kearney fully engages the reader in this very fine coming-of-age novel."   KAREN HESSE

"Kearney is a deft magician, sensitively weaving scenes and histories, lively conversation and internal reckoning into a warm world of relationships. Her poems...feel comfortably vernacular, while embodying a surprising number of poetic forms.... This book is a generous gift."
NAOMI SHIHAB NYE

"Wonderfully written.... Its observations of others and of the narrator herself strike me as honest, filled with the truth of the situation in which Lizzie finds herself. The form is also true—poetry and commentary, both intense and personal."   PAULA FOX

"An exquisite novel about a girl caught in an emotional storm of grief and yearning....told through Lizzie's pitch-perfect poems and journal entries.... inventive, heartbreaking, and transforming."
LABAN CARRICK HILL

PRAISE FOR *The Secret of Me*

"An amazing story...[that] speaks to anyone who has ever asked the questions 'Who am I?' and 'Who will I become?'"   JACQUELINE WOODSON

"Strong feelings are conveyed in a few words, carefully chosen for the strongest emotional impact. A special book filled with insight."
KLIATT

"...just plain touching, pulling the reader in and allowing one to feel what the character feels.... [A] tenderly written book that is definitely for the adopted teen but can be enjoyed by all others."   *VOYA*

"A unique and first-rate offering."   *KIRKUS REVIEWS* (starred)

Also by Meg Kearney

Contents

THE GIRL IN THE MIRROR

Just When I Thought I Had It All Figured Out . . .
The Turn

An Introduction by Lizzie McLane

There was a time, not all that long ago, when I wouldn't tell anyone this: four months after I was born, my mother gave me up for adoption. Sometimes this fact makes me feel sad, but I'm not embarrassed anymore to say it or worried that someone might judge me. More often now, I feel proud that I'm adopted, proud of how my family came to be formed.

Here's how I think of it. When I came into this world, my life took a 90-degree turn. For nine months up until that day, I had been an unborn baby, all curled up in my mother's womb. She and I were traveling down some road, going everywhere together. Maybe when we hit a bump, she'd rub her big belly to calm me. Maybe she sang songs, thinking it would fill our trip with joy. Maybe we had long talks, with her doing all the saying and me doing all the listening. Then came the moment when I emerged from that safe place inside her and came up yelling and gasping for air. That day, we hit The Turn. My mother went left, into the unknown distance—and I went right, into foster care.

My mother—my birth mother—wasn't married. That's not a surprise, but I learned it for certain only earlier this year, just before I graduated from high school. Obviously nobody—her parents or grandparents—jumped in when they learned she was pregnant and said, "_____" [insert unknown name here], "we're going to help make it possible for you to raise that child yourself. No mother should have to give up her baby for adoption." No, nothing like that happened. For whatever reason she couldn't raise me, though I think she wanted to—when I was born, I was put in foster care until she made up her mind for sure. It took her four months to sign the papers and officially give me away.

I stayed in foster care for only five months total. Then I lucked out. The greatest people I could ever imagine adopted me. They brought me from New York City, where I was born, to live with them in this little town north of there, called New Hook, on the Hudson River. One amazing thing I've known most of my life is that as my new parents—Margaret and Patrick McLane—drove down to the City that day to pick me up, they decided to name me Elizabeth Ann. When they got to the New York Foundling (my adoption agency) and announced this to the social worker, she just about fell off her chair. Elizabeth Ann was the name my birth mother had already given me.

I'm not the only child my parents took in. Before me, they adopted my sister Kate—she graduated from the C.I.A. (no, she's not a spy—that's the Culinary Institute of America) and my brother Bob, who's in college with no idea what he'll do when he graduates next year. I hope he doesn't worry about that too much; as Dad said, the main thing college does is teach you how to think.

Neither Kate nor Bob likes to talk about being adopted. But these days, I do enough talking about it for all of us. Or, I should say, I write—reading and writing poems is how I try to make sense out of life. When I was fourteen and starting to think about searching for my birth mother, I wrote a series of poems that I called *The Secret of Me*. When Kate and Bob read it, I thought this huge dam would break and all of their hidden longings and fears and wonderings about where they come from would spill out. But that was just my fantasy. I've come to realize that adoptees have to follow their gut instincts when it comes to this stuff—some of us know, deep down, that we can't live without knowing about our past, our truth; some of us know just as strongly that it's best for us to stay focused on the present, and not worry about whatever happened years ago.

The Secret of Me did work some magic on Mom and Dad. Mom read it in one sitting, planted in her chair in the living room. Dad read a few poems each night just before he went to sleep. As they read, the iceberg called "adoption" that had been squatting frozen between us suddenly melted. They understood, finally, that my wondering who my birth parents are has nothing to do with how much I love them. If I didn't love my family, I never could have written those poems in *The Secret of Me*. So at least after that, the three of us could talk more openly about how we felt, and Mom and Dad even promised they'd help me search for my birth mother when I was a senior in high school. I agreed that seventeen would be a good age to begin, because I'd nearly be an adult and ready to take on just about anything. So I thought.

I was wrong about a lot of things back then, which feels like a lifetime ago. I thought I was traveling down this road with my family and friends—all in the same caravan of cars—with everyone I love beside me or zipping along close behind. I thought what lay ahead was all mapped out. But sometimes you're traveling along a road, as happy as can be, and without warning it takes a 90–degree turn. That turn comes up so fast you almost skid out of control, almost fly off a cliff. Then seconds later you're in a completely different place. You look around, dazed and freaked out, and realize that not everyone who'd been with you made the turn. Someone is missing. The new road ahead is dark; you have no idea where it's heading. All at once your big plans—going to college, searching for your birth mother—are instead a big question mark.

It was April. I was counting the days until my high school graduation. My parents had kept their promise; a letter arrived in the mail from my adoption agency, marking my first step toward searching for my birth mother. But later that same day, my father died. That's when the road not only took a dark turn, but it also disappeared for a while. I was lost. Maybe I was crazy. I did some stupid things and reached a point where I barely recognized myself anymore. But I kept writing poems, kept writing in my journal, and little by little the road grew a little brighter. I collected some of those poems and journal entries and put them together to tell a story. I call it *The Girl in the Mirror.*

Prologue

It was the summer I nearly lost
everything: my charm necklace,
my best friends, my mind, my
shoes, my self-respect, my soul.
Not necessarily in that order.
And for a while, none of it
seemed to matter, because
that spring I'd already lost
the most precious thing of all.

First Poem Since the World Changed

This is no ordinary bench—park bench, picnic bench, cobbler's
bench, bench on either side of a basketball court or baseball
dugout. This is a marble bench, what Dad wanted instead
of a headstone. *I'll have a bench,* he used to say, *so when
you visit you'll stay awhile—drink coffee, have a sandwich,
tell me all the news. It'll be peaceful, and the place has great
views.* Dad would agree it's the perfect place to write a poem
after a long silence, after they laid his body here and the world
changed. I'd write here every day if I could. There's not a soul
around who can say this poem isn't any good.

What Metaphors Are For

(Early May, senior year, high school)

I haven't written anything since
it happened—poems, I mean, or
those "practicing to be a novelist"
pieces I used to write all the time
in my journal. Mrs. Wohl
has been hovering over me

for weeks, like a mother bird
checking her sickly fledgling
in the nest. Then this afternoon
I leave my jacket on my chair
in her classroom, and when
I rush back to get it, she stops

hovering, comes in for a landing.
"Lizzie?" I freeze, hand on my jacket—
it's so warm today, I shouldn't
have bothered. I look at her,
guessing what she'll say. I used to
show her poems, back when,

before. "Lizzie, have you written
anything lately? Want to share?"
I shake my head. I want to *run*.
"You haven't written anything, or
just don't want to share it?"
She's persistent, as always.

"Neither," I say, pulling my jacket
close, as if it's a protective friend.
"What's the point?" I say.
"What's the point?" she echoes,
adding, "You were the one who
told me how poetry helped you

make sense of life." "Oh. *Life,*"
I say, too snotty, but oh well.
That stops her for a second.
"Lizzie—" she has that
I'm-worried-about-you look—
"It will help you sort out

how you *feel.*" My heart shrinks
like it's drying up. My throat
tightens. The jacket has turned
life preserver. *"Feel?"* I blurt—
"You want to know how I *feel?*"
I'm nearly yelling, but she says

"Yes." Patiently. Softly.
"This is what it feels like"—
I'm shaking—"It feels like
a shotgun blast through my chest.
My chest is riddled—filled with
holes. My chest is blasted

with *holes.*" The jacket slips
to the floor as if it's fainted.
Mrs. Wohl puts her hand
on my shoulder. "Well,"
she finally sighs. *"That's*
what I call a metaphor!"

I smile, then the tears come—
a rush, a waterfall.

Her Again

(Early May, English class)

The day after the "metaphor incident,"
Ms. Wohl asks me to stay after class.
I sit with my head in a book of poems
by Sharon Olds until everyone clears out.

"Good book?" Ms. Wohl wants to know.
"Depressing. Really good and depressing,"
I say, thinking, *I wish I could write like that.*
Ms. Wohl settles herself at the desk

next to mine, where Cornelius usually sits.
She wants to know how my mother is,
apologizes for not having asked earlier.
"She's quiet," I say. "She stopped painting."

I don't add how she perks up when people
visit, though fewer stop by now. I don't say
how she puts on a happy voice when people call—
even for my sister Kate and brother Bob—

how it's all an act that only I see. I don't
mention the piles of unopened mail.
The dinners we make and barely touch.
"It's about now that people think

you should be over it," says Ms. Wohl,
staring not at me but out the window.
"The funeral's over, they've sent cards
and casseroles, several weeks have gone by—"

"Five. Five weeks," I say bluntly. "Five
weeks," she repeats, "and they've all gone
back to their lives and think you should, too."
I don't say anything. I can't go back

to a life that isn't. "It's going to take
a *long time,* Lizzie. And that's okay.
It's *normal.* Some of your friends will
get that. Some won't." (*Most don't,*

I think.) "But if you need to talk, you can
call me, okay? Or e-mail." She's looking
at me again, but I stare at my book.
"You're a very good writer, Lizzie,"

she says. "I hope you'll send me some
poems now and then." I hesitate, then
look at her and promise, "I will,"
though it feels too much like a lie.

Journal Entry #2102: There Goes the Sun

(Looking back at April 1 of this year)

I imagine that Tuesday he got up early, same time as Mom—
6 a.m., like always—and she made coffee while he walked down
our hill to fetch the paper and the mail (which I should have picked
up on Monday afternoon but forgot). He was already in his dark
blue suit.

She made him toast and he slathered it with margarine and
blackberry jelly. I picture them sitting, sipping coffee while he read
the headlines out loud to her, stopping after a few minutes to tell
her how beautiful she looked with the sun streaming in on her
dark coppery hair. She probably got up then to pour more coffee,
laughing, when he took her hand and pulled her onto his lap. I bet
he kissed her before he told her about the meeting he had sched-
uled after school. How he'd asked his teachers to come prepared to
talk openly about how the year had gone, now that it was winding
down. Then he said, "Wasn't that great, seeing Lizzie in the card
shop, a working girl now, all grown up."

That's when I walked in, probably looking sleepy but already
showered and dressed. Mom jumped to her feet and Dad stood up,
too. He told me I look great in pink, then slipped an envelope from
the top of a small stack of mail.

"This came for you," he explained, handing me the envelope then
gently holding my arms. He looked into my eyes, said, "We'll talk
about this later, all right? We're glad you've taken this step, Lizzie."
Mom was nodding. "We'll look at it together, tonight, if you want."

Mom nodded again, smiling, a little stiff but just a little. I stared
at the envelope's return address: New York Foundling. The non-identifying information about my birth mother. It had been six weeks
and two days since Mom and Dad and I had filled out the form, and
they had signed and mailed it for me. I needed to sit down.

Dad kissed me on the cheek and said, "It'll be fine, *you'll* be
fine—I know you will. So take a deep breath and remember that." I
must have looked doubtful. "If I could take the day off, I would—"
he started, and I said, "No, Dad, it's okay. The principal can't take
the day off! I'll want to be alone when I read it, anyway. I think
I'll wait until after school. I can't read this and *then* go to school!"

He put his hands on my shoulders and said, "I'll be busy until after four. Call me if you need to—if I can't answer I'll call you back as soon as I can." "I'll be home all day, too," added Mom in her helpful voice. He turned to her, kissed her on the lips, and squeezed her hand. "Love you," she said.

Then he was out the door, in his car, waving as he pulled down the driveway. Off to work. And he never came back.

The Day My Father Died

I thought it was a joke.
They called me out of class—
Mom's voice said Dad was dead.
I dropped my phone. They sent me home.

They called me out of class—
said I should call my mom.
I dropped my phone. They sent me home
where everything was surreal—

They said I should call Mom.
But her voice was strange, a stranger's.
Everything was surreal—
our house was filled with people.

Mom's voice was strange, a stranger's—
"Lizzie," she said, and hugged me.
Our house was filled with people
who wanted to hug me, too.

"Lizzie," Mom said, and hugged me—
we stood that way a long time.
Other people wanted to hug me, too—
I wanted *them* to leave us alone.

We stood that way a long time.
Neither of us could cry.
I wanted everyone to leave us alone—
I wanted this to be a bad dream.

Neither of us could cry—
crying would mean it was true.
I wanted this to be a bad dream
but I heard *heart attack* and *car*—

crying would mean it was true:
Dad had pulled the car over, he knew—
but I heard *heart attack* and *car*
and wanted to shout, "You're all lying!"

Dad had pulled the car over. He knew
it was his heart, exploding—
I wanted to shout, "You're all lying!"
Where was Dad? He'd show them

it wasn't his heart, exploding.
It was April first, a trick!
Where was Dad? He'd show them.
He'd walk through that door.

It was April first, a trick!
Mom's voice said Dad was dead.
He couldn't walk through that door.
I thought it was a joke.

Dad's Wake

I don't remember much of those hours
at the funeral home: the rows of chairs,
glimmer of candles, how all the flowers
made me choke. Mom, Kate, Bob, and I stood there
in front of that casket as people streamed
by like a river. We shook their hands, said
"Thanks" or let them do all the talking—we
were in a trance. *In that box, Dad is dead,*
I kept saying in my head, *so why do*
they call this a "wake"? I thought such strange things
while I hugged friends and all those people who
knew Dad and loved him and wanted to sing
his praises. My head ached. My hands were cold.
Mom, dressed in black, looked thin—and so old.

Dad's Funeral

Bob drove us to the church and walked in first
with Mom on his arm. Kate and I followed
close behind, trying not to see the hearse
parked out front. I gripped Kate's hand and swallowed
some venomous thing rising in my throat.
"In the name of the Father, and the Son . . ."
Father Dan began, and by the first note
of "Amazing Grace" there was not one
dry eye in the place except for Mom's. Stiff
with grief, she leaned on Bob. I held Kate's hand,
which was cold like mine. People sang as if
their hearts would break. *But mine will never mend,*
I thought. *Amazing Grace, how sweet the sound,*
we sang again, when they put him in the ground.

Journal Entry #2103: Irish Funeral Party

I. Mom sits on the couch with Kate on one side and Toshi's mom Isabel on the other. I can see Mom's lips move now and then but can't hear a word because the entire town of New Hook seems to be crammed in our house. There's a mess of people I recognize, and some I swear I've never seen before, but they act as if they know who I am. Those are the ones who like to hug the most. I learn to steer clear of them, especially women with really huge boobs holding empty wine glasses.

It's impossible to hear anyone except whoever's within a four-foot radius, which means I hear Cathy, who took the train up from the city the second I called her, and of course Jan and Toshi, who've been so great about calling and coming over, and even Deb, who I'd kind of lost track of in tenth grade but turns out to be true-blue in times of trouble. And Barb, who went cheerleader on us and I've only seen at games for the past two years even though she was still always nice and said hi. Toshi told me that Peter and Robert are somewhere around, too, which turns out to be in the garage hanging with Bob and his buddies.

I'm glad Peter is with them. Even though we broke up a couple of years ago, we're friends, but still . . . I think he wants me to know he's near if I need him. Cathy says he's just here for the beer.

As if the whole thing isn't surreal enough, Mrs. Wiler, that old Spanish teacher, comes up to me in the living room chattering about how she never realized how tall I am until she saw me with my family in the front pew of the church, and there I was, taller than everyone, including Bob. I don't even *try* to fake a smile, but turn to Cathy and the rest of my girls to change the subject. Cathy and Jan—my two best friends who also happen to be adopted—give me a secret, knowing look. But Mrs. Wiler, always a bit thick, keeps talking. She insists how different I *really do look* compared with everybody else in my family, and is that a recessive gene, or—she says, touching me on the arm like we're buds sharing a joke, because obviously I *need* to laugh—she teeters and tee-hees at her own, lame, tired line: *"Or was it the cable guy?"*

At this I open my mouth but nothing comes out but "*You—*"
At that very second, Cathy grabs my arm, swings me around like
her dance partner, and hauls me through the crowd before I can
recover myself enough to say the word at the tip of my tongue....
all's a swirl and suddenly we're standing in the kitchen with the
moms pulling steaming casseroles from the oven and arranging
cheese and crackers on plates.

"BEAST!" I scream. Then out of my mouth comes this hoarse
kind of giggle-choke sound. Everybody stops whatever it is they're
saying and doing and stares at us.

Next thing I know, Cathy has my arm again and is yanking me
out the kitchen door to the backyard. She starts to laugh and then
I start and we laugh until it hurts enough to cry.

II. Blur of bodies, blur of faces, blur
of voices—my mind is a blur;
my head, numb from too much
too much. I slip onto the front
porch, chill of air & stone steps
a place to rest. Everyone
who's coming today is probably
inside, chatting in the living room
or drinking a beer with Bob
in the garage or washing dishes
among the kitchen gossips.
No one will bother me here,
no one will want a long hug
or tell me how strong
I am. I don't want to be
strong. I just want my life
back. I just want to zap
a magic wand and wrap
my arms around Dad's
neck. If only Dad had—

what? A glut of what-ifs.
If onlys. A car door slams
and my heart leaps—
no, not Dad. But Tim.
Tim Ryan, who recited
"Clarinet" in English
class, the newish boy who
might not love poetry as much
as I do but who has Terrance
Hayes by heart and walks the halls
swinging an imaginary
golf club. Who I hear plays
guitar; who may be one
of the oddest people by far:
poetry + music =
GOLF? A mystery, Tim,
who now sits beside me,
extends a yellow rose
with a shaky brown hand.
"Yellow means friendship,"
he says, but the flower's
perfume is funeral home
& church and I pull another
tissue from the box I now
carry everywhere. I don't
care that I've become this
fountain of salty water
and snot. Not that Tim
seems to care, either—
we haven't even said hello.
We sit together, breathing.
Then, after a while, he says,
"My mother died when I
was a baby. Two days old.
She had an aneurism.

A blood vessel burst in her
brain. They say it was over
in seconds flat." No words
come to me. I stick my nose
in the flower. He says, "I never
knew her. I miss her every day."
I look at Tim now. He gazes out
at the grass, loosens his tie.
Then he looks at me. I've never
felt so *seen.* If I could dive into
the dark of those eyes—maybe
the worst would be past us
by the time I surfaced. But my head
is heavy; it's on his shoulder.
Just when I thought all the planks
of the dam inside me had burst,
I feel another heave and splinter,
then give way. A while later
I blurt, "I'm getting your shirt
wet." He puts his hand on mine
and says, "I like it like that."

It's a Long Way to Normal

(A week after Dad's funeral)

It's time to go back to school, back
        to normal, Mom says.

It's time to go back to work, back
        to books, to poems, to eating,
        sleeping, hanging with friends.

It's time to go back to smiling, singing,
        dreaming about college, and boys,
        back to the girl I was before.

But I say it's time to be real, time to get the clue:
        that girl will never be back, never
        feel the same—
        and Mom, neither will you.

Haunted by the Foundling Letter
Or, *Maybe This Whole Search Thing Is a Bad Idea*

Open me! Open me! cries the letter
on my desk. I pick it up, put it down.
Cathy says knowing what's in it is better
than not. Jan says, "She's not gonna come pound
on your door—if you want to find her, what
are you waiting for?" Mom says, "I'm not your
Dad, but I'm here when you're ready." I shut
my ears—what if I knocked on *her* door,
and she slammed it in my face? I lost her
once already. And now I've lost my dad.
Parents have a way of disappearing, pure
and simple. I'd feel more sure if I had
a crystal ball to show me the future.
Would it say I'm nuts to open that letter?

The letter kept whispering from the corner of my desk: "Aren't you the least bit curious? How can you stand not knowing what I know?"

Even Mom couldn't take it anymore. "When *are* you going to open that letter from the Foundling?" she said this morning. "Reading it doesn't mean you have to go any further. You can just find out what it says, and let that be it—you don't have to actually search if you don't want to. This can be the next step, and the last."

I stared at her a full minute, then said, "Yeah. . . . YEAH!"

"I'm here if you need me!" she called as I stomped up the stairs to my room. *But if I freak out,* I thought, *Dad would be the one to calm me down.*

I lit a candle, then fought the urge to throw up. When I felt calmer, I lit three more candles, placed them around me on the floor, and tore open the envelope.

When the room started to spin, I was glad I was already on the floor. I read it twenty-two times. A voice in my head repeated, *This is* your *life,* her *life . . .* trying to make it feel real. Trying to connect the words on that page to me, Lizzie McLane. I couldn't cry, but I think I made some strange noises. Maybe I was talking out loud. I could hear Mom outside my door. "Are you okay? You want me to come in?" "No," I said. "I'm okay. I'll be okay."

Later, I found Mom in the kitchen and let her read the letter. When she handed it back to me she said, "I love you, Lizzie. And your birth mother did, too. I wish I could take away your pain—I wish I could explain why she had to do what she did—but I can't." There were dark smudges under Mom's eyes like little bruises, and yet she sat straight as a pencil. I put my hand on her cheek, but she took it in her two hands and held it as she continued. "All I can say is it was *her* love that made you part of this family. If not for her telling the Foundling, very specifically, what she wanted for you— who knows, but you might not have ended up with us. I'll always be grateful, endlessly grateful to her for that."

We both cried then. It was a soggy afternoon.

Journal Entry #2104.1

(Evening)

I'm retyping what the letter says here—in case I ever lose it I'll have another copy. (The world hasn't stopped spinning yet. I've read it eighty-seven times total so far.)

Dear Mr. and Mrs. McLane:

This letter is being sent to you in response to your request for non-identifying information concerning your daughter, Elizabeth.

Elizabeth's birth mother was nineteen years old, unmarried, Catholic, and in good health at the time of Elizabeth's birth. Her birth mother's hair and eyes were brown. She was 5'9" tall and weighed 140 pounds. She had one year of college and planned to finish her degree.

Her maternal grandparents were from Scotland. They were also in good health at the time of Elizabeth's birth.

Elizabeth's birth father was twenty-five years old and 6'3" tall. He was college-educated and of French descent, though his family had been in the United States for several generations. He was in good health; there is no record concerning the health of his parents.

Two months before Elizabeth was born, her birth mother came to us seeking counseling and support services. She wanted very much to give her baby the life she thought she deserved, but feared her own fragile financial situation and lack of college degree would hinder her child's chances. The birth mother's relationship with the birth father had ended before she knew she was pregnant, and she decided not to involve him.

At first, Elizabeth's birth mother spoke of the idea of adoption mechanically, without feeling. She spent many hours in the Foundling chapel, crying and praying for help with her decision.

At birth, Elizabeth weighed 6 pounds, 14 ounces. She cried immediately. When she was ready for release from the hospital, her birth mother was not yet willing to sign the necessary papers and Elizabeth was placed in foster care.

Although she was pronounced a healthy baby, Elizabeth's hypermobility made it necessary for her to have frequent medical check-ups during her first few months. Her birth mother met Elizabeth at the doctor's office each time she had an appointment.

By December, her birth mother had come to terms with the fact that she was not able to provide the life she wanted Elizabeth to have. She signed the surrender papers on December 14. As you know, Elizabeth was placed with you as her adoptive parents on January 10.

If you have any questions or concerns, feel free to call the Adoption Services number at the bottom of this letter.

Sincerely,

Sophie Fedorowicz
MSEd., LCSW

Journal Entry #2105

I don't think I slept all night. At 3 a.m. I gave up and read the letter a few more times.

Surrendered. She *surrendered,* as if she were an army of one and was surrounded by enemies. She waved the white flag in December . . . Well, thank freakin' God. I wouldn't have it any other way. Right?

Journal Entry #2105.1
(Same day)

I'm not Irish. I am Scottish and French. French! French?

Why didn't I take French instead of Spanish? I speak NO French.

Dad spoke a little French. We'd have so much to talk about if—

Journal Entry #2105.2
(Ditto)

Wikipedia definition: "hypermobility: (also called extreme-flex, Hypermobility Syndrome, Benign Joint Hypermobility Syndrome or hyperlaxity) describes joints that stretch farther than is normal. For example, some hypermobile people can bend their thumbs backwards to their wrists, bend their knee joints backwards, put their leg behind the head or perform other contortionist acts. It can affect a single joint or multiple joints throughout the body."

No wonder I can bend my thumb to touch my wrist. I used to be able to wrap both legs behind my neck! Bob still calls me Gumby sometimes, after that cartoon character who can bend in every direction because he's made of rubber.

Mom says they had to give me special stretching exercises until I was a year old. Why didn't she ever tell me that before?!?

I will grow up to be tall and average weight. Thank God.

Journal Entry #2105.3

(Night)

She believed in God.

Why didn't her parents help?? She was lonely. Alone.

He doesn't even know I *exist*. And he's French.

She made the right decision. That's what I'd tell her.

Journal Entry #2106

She didn't want to give me up. She might be registered with one of those places on the Internet, in case I want to find her. Cathy gave me a list of all the sites—"registries"—where people who are adopted *and* people who gave up kids for adoption can type in their names (or their kids' names) and birth dates and stuff, and try to find each other that way, try to find a match. Kind of like online dating, only different.

I've now read that letter 103 times.

Jan thinks it's so cool I arrived in New Hook on her birthday, January 10. But, she asked, didn't I know all along that it was my adoption day? She said some families make a big deal out of adoption day, like it's a second birthday. Hers is January 11—she was just a day old—and her family didn't celebrate it, either. (I have no idea why I didn't ask my parents about this years ago. It didn't even dawn on me to ask what day I arrived—me, who is obsessed with this stuff!) Anyway, it's now a special day for both of us, Jan said.

Mom says she honestly forgot about giving me the stretching exercises, it was so long ago. I'm thinking the double-jointed thing could be genetic.

I wish Dad were here.

Journal Entry #2106.1

Have hardly slept or eaten since I opened The Letter. Mom says maybe this was all too soon, though she knows there's no going back. Still, she thinks I should go ahead and have my party. I told her I don't feel like it anymore, and besides, *everyone* is having a graduation party. She said, "Right. Including you." Whatever.

The Letter doesn't say much about my birth father. Cathy said her non-identifying information said even less about hers. Her letter was just a couple of sentences long!

Part of me wants to go to bed and stay there for a month. If only I could get all this chatter in my head to stop.

Imagine, she was nineteen when she had me! That's just a year older than I am, almost! Now she's thirty-seven. It seems so unreal. Like a movie starring unknown actors, one of whom is me.

They call it *surrendering*.

Back to Work

"Hello! Cards and gifts!" is how we answer the phone
at The Hello Shop. "Hello!" we have to greet everyone
who walks in the door looking for a birthday card,
picture frame, bone-china vase from England, or any

of various dust collectors people call "collectibles."
"Hello, Lizzie McLane, welcome back," says
Mrs. Bernstein on my first Saturday at work
in weeks. At Dad's funeral, she told me to take all

the time I need, that "the girls" would cover my hours
until I was ready. *Ready?* I thought at the time, *I'm not
ready for anything.* "Welcome back," says Sharon
as I lock my purse in a drawer underneath the register.

"Hey, Lizzie," Jackie calls from behind the Mother's
Day cards. (*Mother's Day! Crap! I forgot.*)
I try my best to smile at everyone, but something's
wrong with my mouth. Sharon's about to leave me

at the register, but Mrs. Bernstein says today
we're all switching places: Sharon's on the register,
Jackie's covering the floor (dusting the Hummel
figurines and hard-selling Lenox china to ladies

wearing too much perfume). I'm in cards, which
means straightening, replacing missing envelopes,
filling empty spots, recording which ones need to be
re-ordered. In other words, she sticks me where

I don't have to talk much, where I can hide. This
seems like a great idea until I find myself staring
at the birthday cards for Father, Dad, Daddy . . .
I'm so inconsolable, Mrs. Bernstein sends me home.

After

(Last winter, end of basketball season)

After the final game of the season,
after Dad took Margo & me out
to celebrate (dinner at Del Rossi's),
after chocolate cake and our bad joke
contest ("What's worse than a worm
in an apple?"

                        "Half a worm!"),
after laughing so hard I swallowed
my after-dinner mint whole, after
we drove Margo home, after we
pulled up the driveway and Dad cut
the Subaru's engine and I reached
for the door handle, Dad said,
Wait. He pulled a yellow gift bag
from behind my seat. For my champ,
he said. It was dark but I could see
he was smiling. "But I only made first
string because Tiara broke her leg,"
I protested, searching for the button
overhead to turn on a light. I knew
he didn't care about first string, second
string—he was always there, nearly
every game. In the bag was a box.
In the box was a silver chain,
and from it dangled a silver basketball,
about the size of a quarter. "It's *gorgeous*,"
I said, flipping it over in my hand.
It was inscribed: *Lizzie / My Star /
Love / Dad.* I couldn't speak; I just
put it on. I wear it everywhere. After
he died, I swore I'd never take it off.

Skinny

Mom's gotten skinny fast. Even Bob notices
when he comes home for the weekend from college.
Holy crap, he says to me when we're on the back porch
steps, out of earshot. We're going to lose her next,
he says, if she doesn't start eating. I watch an ant tug
a crumb across the bottom step. And you—he jabs me,
not hard, with his elbow—you, too, Lizzie. You're nearly
as skinny as Mom. You two on a hunger strike? I try
to smile, touching my necklace as if the charm might be
a talisman against Mom's death, against Bob even *saying*
she might be next. Bob, Kate, they're on their own, out
of this house with all of its new silences and empty spaces.
Mom and I stumble around here as if it's always dark
and someone snuck in and rearranged the furniture.
We don't talk much, but we do like to hug. We forget
to eat, or we cook pasta and make a big salad and then sit
down at the table without appetites. We take a few bites
and put the rest in the fridge. She sits among her paints
and brushes, staring at an empty canvas. I hold a pen
in my hand, stare at a blank sheet of paper. Even reading
is hard. I'll get to the bottom of a page and realize I have
no idea what I just read, and have to start over. As for
The Letter— all that stuff feels like it's about someone
else's life. That's why I keep reading it over and over;
maybe it'll all start to feel real. Poems are the only things
that seem to make sense. So I read them. Writing them
is another story. Like diving into water so murky I can't
see, so deep it feels as if my heart will explode. Such
a relief to come up for air. Then I dive again.

Have you heard a word I said? asks Bob when he sees me
staring into space. Then I feel his elbow again, even more
gently this time. He looks blurry through my tears.
He puts his arm around me. He's crying, too.

Mother's Day Poem I Decide Not to Give Mom

It's a mother's love we honor today—
mothers & grandmothers, living & dead—
for what's a mother's love when given away

but a bright box of crayons (no blue-black, no gray),
a garden of flowers, lime-yellow & red.
It's a mother's love we honor today,

a love that gives shelter to orphans & strays,
that makes sure we are cared for, sheltered, & fed.
What's a mother's love when given away

without expectation of rewards or presents or pay—
whose only fear is losing you, which fills her with dread.
It's such a mother's love we honor today—

both the mother who holds you & the one who couldn't stay,
the one you live with; the one who lives in your head.
It's two mothers' love that I honor today—
(though what *is* a mother's love when she gives you away?)

Journal Entry #2107: Not the Same

No freakin' way am I telling Peter about getting the non-identifying information. Picture this: he & I are at James Bard State Park, our old hangout, sitting on the same plaid blanket we used to sit on all the time four years ago when we were going out. I'm reminiscing about the old days, when Dad & Gram were healthy, kinda. Bob and Kate still lived at home. Mom was painting a lot. Cathy still lived in New Hook. I was four years away from being old enough to search for my birth mother; I hadn't even told Peter that I'm adopted—

"Remember?" I say, "And now—" "Look!" interrupts Peter. "A female cardinal. I bet the male—he's *really* red—is close." The bird's out of sight already. Peter starts chattering about cardinals being good luck or something. I might as well have been saying "Blah blah blah blah blah . . . "

I go quiet, start playing with my charm necklace, thinking how Mom actually asked me about The Letter—how it makes me feel, what my thoughts are about taking another step toward searching. She's worried I've taken on too much, too soon after Dad. She can tell I'm not sleeping very well. How can I? Every detail of that letter is still flying around inside my head like a bat, bumping into things.

Peter is talking about what dorm he wants to be in this fall at Miami, how his brother Sam gave him all these tips about pizza places, when I spot the male cardinal.

He looks like he just stepped out of Mom's box of paints. I'd love to see her pull out a brush and cut a swath of cardinal across a white canvas.

"Hey, is anybody in there?" Peter's looking at me with that I'm-gonna-cheer-you-up-now look. He puts his arm around me. "Everything's gonna be okay," he says. I don't answer. It's something people say.

"When my Nana died, I was sad for months," Peter says. I pull away, look at him hard. "I'm still not over losing Gram," I say slowly, my voice a little shaky, "and that was two years ago. But this is nothing, *nothing* like that. You can't compare—"

I have to stop. My throat hurts. I want to punch something. "I'm sorry," Peter says, but he knows better than to try to put his arm around me again. It looks as if he's going to say something else, but then thinks better of it. I wish he would just say that I'm right: he has no idea how I feel. That he can't "fix" it. We don't talk much walking home. When we reach my house, I don't invite him in.

Without

After a poem by Donald Hall

Without his arm around my shoulder without his voice without
kisses on my forehead without laughter at the dinner table
without his prayer before a meal without stink of cigars without
his hands on the wheel without bright red socks without fiddles
and pennywhistles without a cozy fire on winter nights without
singing without corny jokes without big leather gloves without boat
shoes and shorts without neckties without principal without
bird calls without red hair fading to gray without gardens without
goofy grins without barbecues in the rain without Father's Day
cards without banana splits without guidance without Danny Boy
& Mrs. Murphy's Chowder without It's a Grand Old Flag without
Daddy's Little Girl without extra pepper hold the salt without
handkerchiefs without books on the floor around his chair.
Empty chair.

The Night Before Graduation

(Late June)

I slide into the driver's seat of Dad's
Subaru, that car he said was so safe

with its dual airbags and all-wheel drive. I
glide my hand over the stick shift, thinking

back to being sixteen, such a dork when
he taught me to drive. He was so patient

when I stalled out, ground the gears, slammed the brakes
too hard, giving us both a jolt. I run

a finger around the ring his coffee
mug left in the cup holder. The car smells

like cigars—he smoked them only here, when
he was alone—and peppermint. I pull

one from its plastic bag, pop it in my
mouth, stare at the note pad, his handwriting:

"Tues—9 a.m." and "Call G." Caressing
the steering wheel, the dash, radio dials—

I breathe deep. Mr. Z said in science
class that we're all breathing the same air that

ancient people breathed—cavemen and Plato,
Jesus and Shakespeare, Walt Whitman and Walt

Disney. I take a deeper breath, hold it
in my lungs. *I'm holding you, Dad,* I think.

When I wake, my neck feels stiff. It's morning.
A blanket covers me. In my right hand,
I clutch Dad's glasses; in my left, his pen.

Commencement

Did we process two by two like animals
into the ark? Did Jan hold my hand,

as if it were dark, and she was the one
with the light? Did we sit upright

through an hour of speeches? Did Jan
reach for that beach ball sailing over

our heads, nail it flying toward Tim
Ryan, who punched it higher than

heaven? Did Jan pull me to my feet
so I'd follow her to the stage? Did

Mr. LaPage shake my hand, give me
my diploma? Did I wave it over my

head, wanting to show Mom? Is that
when I looked for Dad, just before

we threw our mortarboard hats
into the air—a flock of white, startled

birds soaring this way and that?
Did I shout? Did I cry? Did I care?

Reunion Fantasy #1003

(Saturday morning, Hello Shop)

Every time the door jingles open, something in me stirs.
The way I react, you'd think I'm under a spell.
This could be it, could be the day, it could be her

walking into the store. I know it sounds absurd.
What are the chances it's my birth mother ringing that bell?
Every time the door jingles open, something in me stirs,

and I'm pulled in that direction like a fish to a lure.
I try to resist, try to act kind of cool, but—well,
this *could* be it, *could* be the day, it *could* be her

until it's clear it's not—Hello, may I help you, sir?
I say then with a smile, and do my job: I sell.
Still, every time the door jingles open, something in me stirs

that feels older than time. My heart flits like a bird
in a cage; my longing rattles the bars of its cell.
This could be it, could be the day, it could be her

strolling in, wearing a blue blouse, sunhat, fur
coat. If it is, I know I'll somehow be able to tell.
Every time the door jingles open, something in me stirs—
this could be it, could be the day, it *could* be her.

The Graduation Party: A Story in Poetry & Prose

(Last day of June)

I. Warming Up for a Party I Don't Want Anymore

Cathy takes an early train from the city to help me get things ready. The minute she gets in my car, all we talk about is The Letter. She says being half French makes me exotic. She wonders, too, why my birth mother's parents didn't help her so she could keep me, but agrees—my birth mother obviously had big plans for me and what my life would be, and thank God she finally signed those papers, or I wouldn't be here right now.

The adoption support group will help me figure out the next step toward searching, Cathy says. I point to show her that the old Dairy Queen is now a flower shop. What's the big hurry? I feel like a snowwoman, frozen while a storm of grief and confusion rages around me. I can't see for all the ice and wind and "what ifs." How am I supposed to search when nothing will stand still, nothing is clear anymore? Dad was supposed to help me with this. He was supposed to be here.

We get back to my house and who's in the front yard waiting? Peter, looking like he's on his way to Hawaii with his loud flowered shirt and shorts. Cathy sighs. I ask him to be the DJ, and he agrees.

Peter spends half an hour running around, plastering paper copies of my graduation photo on everything Scotch tape will stick to—the mailbox, picnic table, poles that hold up the patio roof. I hate that photo, how weirdly sick I look in that stupid white cap. It's like I'm saying, "Go ahead, shoot me." Mom sees me start to tear down a copy taped to the back door and says, "Don't you dare. That's Peter's idea. His *gift*. Leave them." Whatever.

Cathy is chatting away with Mom, describing Stuyvesant, where she finished high school, telling about her trip coming up to Mexico, when my cell phone rings. "It's me, stuck in the shop," says Jan, "Mind if I bring somebody? We'll be there as soon as his car is ready, as soon as we can, okay?" I can hear the smile in Jan's voice. "Who— yeah, of course it's fine—who's the somebody?" I say. "Guess," she says. I don't have the energy. "Surprise me," I say.

Now Peter is down in The Lounge, a basement room that Bob had taken over during his junior year of high school and made into a cushiony lair. I'd set up my (formerly Kate's) stereo there, in case it rained, then ran the wires out through the window—the one that's foundation level, just behind the rhododendron bushes.

The Palisades are blaring their new hit while Cathy, Mom, and I arrange lawn chairs in circles, worrying if we have enough ice and still catching up on Cathy's new life in Manhattan, where her dad has this cool new writing gig; her mom is re-establishing her dental practice. Then two cars pull in the driveway and three more park at the bottom of our hill and all at once we're in Party Mode. Maureen & Margo do a dance-walk up the lawn to the rhythm of the Sugar Bush Band's "Gotta Love It."

II. Ready or Not: Party

"We arrived right on time!" shouts Margo. "You ready to dance, Lizzie?" She puts her arm through mine. "I'd rather be in bed," I murmur. "What are you talking about?" Margo says, gently teasing. I know she senses my sudden nerves, the way she sensed during a basketball game when I'd be under the net, and I sensed when the ball would arrive—we made a killer team, we two, senior year.

Smile, I tell myself, fingering my charm—that's what Dad would advise at this moment. I get teary, quick put on my sunglasses. I'm thinking, I'm going to win an Academy Award for this, as "Oh, hi!" I call, all cheery; and "Hey! It's so cool you could come," I say to a zillion friends—Toshi & Robert (together again for the ninety-ninth time), Cindy, Marion, Jake, even skinnier-than-ever Barb (who can "only stay a minute"), and Deb, who's been so great since Dad ... Mom says, "There must be fifty kids here!" She makes a face of mock horror and escapes into the house. Tanya follows her; a minute later she comes out of the kitchen, a bowl of chips in one hand, a bowl of salsa in the other.

Cornelius heads for the barbecue with a bag of charcoal under his arm. Toshi and Margo were with him a second ago, but seem to have disappeared. Jan still hasn't arrived with her mystery guest, so Cathy and I go searching for our DJ. Hadn't Peter just loaded up the CD player and come outside?

"We can hook up my iPod and not have to worry about music the rest of the night," says Cathy as we weave our way through the maze of people, then adds, "Who's that?" I introduce her to Gabriel and JL, then Tiara. "Geez, you've made a lot of new friends since I left!" she says. We keep moving, looking for Peter. "He's still in love, you know," Cathy says as we take off our sunglasses and head down the basement stairs. "Shhh!" I warn. The air must be 20 degrees cooler in the basement, and there's that slightly moldy smell we just can't get rid of, even with the dehumidifier.

In The Lounge, a whole other party is in full-force—Peter, Robert, Toshi, Deb, and Margo are all laughing, draped over Bob's couches and overstuffed chairs like they're in their own living room. More copies of my graduation photo stare from the walls.

The air in here smells almost sweet, no mold. I'm jittery, but Cathy seems cool, so I try to smile. "We thought you'd never get here," says Peter, coming toward me with those save-the-planet blue eyes. "Wanna drink?" he asks, holding out his plastic cup. Everyone stops to watch. Cathy sees something's up before I do. She grabs Toshi's drink, takes a sip, looks at me. "Spiked." I freeze, the drink still extended in Peter's hand.

I feel nervous, angry, and surprisingly calm all at the same time. I ask, "You spiked the lemonade?" Peter looks at Deb, who says, "I brought us some special—" pointing to a big orange drink thermos, the kind we'd have filled with Gatorade next to the bench at basketball games. "It's okay . . ." says Toshi, unsure. "We're adults," Peter claims, and I raise my right eyebrow as if to say, We are? . . . But I do feel a lot older. I've felt that way since April. And I don't want to seem like Miss Goody-Goody, afraid to have fun.

"So who's the designated driver?" I ask. Cathy plucks two cups from a stack, turns to look at me. "Well, you know I walked," says

Peter. "People can stay at my place. My parents won't care." Cathy, who's staying for the weekend, holds out a cup, tilts her head like she's asking a question. I zip my charm back and forth on its chain, suddenly feeling reckless.

I nod to Cathy, and Deb jumps to her feet. "Let me buy the first round!" Everybody laughs, including me. "Who'd ever guess your Dad owns a bar?" Cathy says as Deb hands us our drinks. I cringe, with a sudden thought of Jan and how upset she'd be—but I push that aside. Peter slides his arm around my shoulder. That feels almost right. Still, he looks like such a nerd in that purple flowered shirt, and he's got a roll of tape sticking out of each pocket of his shorts. Not *nerd*. Dork.

"A toast!" Everybody holds up their glasses. "Here's to friends, old and new," Cathy says, "And to the end of high school!" We all let out a cheer and take a drink. I sip. It *is* good.

I show everyone a closet where we stash the lemonade, and we head back to the party. No one knows our drinks are spiked. No one even suspects, until Jan arrives.

III. Cellar Rat

Here comes the cellar rat, I think
as we spill up the steps to the lawn.
I don't want to feel guilty about
drinking. Mom's probably curled up
on the couch, asleep again, anyway.
Jan doesn't have to know.

. . . What would *she* think? Would
my birth mother be one of those easy-
going parents who lets her kids drink,
at least when they're home? Would she
even *join* us, like some parents do?
Or would she be strict, all about rules?

"Clink," I say, pecking the rim
of my plastic cup to Peter's. "Liz!"
I hear Jan's voice calling me. "Over
here!" She motions from the picnic
table, squashing over so I can sit
with her and her surprise guest—

Tim! Sweet Tim. I tell everyone
that he was the only kid besides me
in Ms. Wohl's class who could name
the Poet Laureate, Forest Jackson.
It's as if I'm hovering over the table,
watching myself flirting, saying,

Girl, you're not very good at it.
Give it up. "Sorry to make Jan late
to your bash," Tim says, standing to give
me a quick hug and make room for Cathy,
who's elbowed Peter out of the way
and stuck to me like icing on cake.

"A gentleman, too," Cathy says to Tim.
"I didn't know *that* about you." *No!* I scream
in my head. *He'll know I e-mailed you . . . !* "Oh?
What *did* you know?" asks Tim with a sly
smile. Heat rushes to my face—or is that
the drink? Then I feel a lush kind of calm.

I peer into my cup. "What kind of black
people," Cathy says, "would name their baby
'Forest'?" She turns to me. "Forest is one
of those white people names I dread, like
'River' or 'Dakota.'" *My birth mother named
me Elizabeth. Mom and Dad named me*

the same. I am really *an Elizabeth,* I think.
Who's ever given the same name twice?
"My sister's name is Dakota," Tim says, his brow
all knit and serious. Everyone freezes. I take
a gulp of lemonade. "Kidding!" Tim declares,
laughing, and everyone busts up. "And you

don't look totally white, either," says Cathy,
with an air only she, who's half black, can pull
off. "I'm half Mexican," answers Tim, his head
high. That explains his dark eyes and gorgeous,
smooth, sun-kissed brown skin. He catches me
staring, flashes a grin. *I'm half French,* I want

to say. *Half Scottish, too. I just found out—*
I down the rest of my drink. "Bark up the right
tree, the cat might come down on his own,"
Cathy says. We all look at her, puzzled. "That
means," I announce, ready with my own joke—
all eyes are on me now, but my mind is mush—

"That means it's time to eat," Peter offers, trying
to save me. Jan eyes me funny. I can't meet
her gaze. *Just call me a cellar rat, Jan,* I think.
"Liz!" calls Cornelius, who's manning the grill.
"We have that kind made outta fake meat!"
he yells, knowing I'm going vegetarian,

like my sister Kate. We all stand up—*Saved
by a veggie burger,* I think, then sit back down.
My head's swirling like a storm in a snow globe.
Does my birth mother eat meat? "Dizzy?"
asks Jan, peering at me. "Yeah, I really need
to eat," I say, and she softens. I've lost a lot

of weight since Dad died. Now I've freed
myself from suspicion by drawing on her vast
sympathy. Ugh. *I am a rat.* "Is this seat
taken?" Peter's back with two plates and two
more lemonades. He plops down next to me
and winks. I whack him playfully on the arm

as Jan walks away. *"She* wouldn't approve
of the lemonade, huh?" I shake my head.
Her dad started drinking when her mom
left, when we were juniors. "Well, you did
look happier than you have in months—"
he touches my arm—"just a little while ago,"

he says. "Nothing wrong with that. Nothing
wrong with letting go a little." He's right.
Dad would want me to relax. Mom, too.
They sometimes let me have a little wine
at dinner. I take a bite of burger, then a long
swig. I feel kind of good, and kind of like a rat.

IV. Jan, Meet Jade

"Who's that Asian girl?" Jan asks, looking over my shoulder. I turn,
spot Jade looking lost by the cooler, and wave her over. "Jade," I tell
Jan. "From group. She's Korean." I think Jan is glad I haven't been
to the adoption support group since—Dad. I suspect she'd like to

go, but bet the idea of spilling all those feelings, like spilling gasoline all over the ground, seems dangerous. Some spark might come out of nowhere and she'd explode.

"Hey!" I give Jade an I'm-glad-you're-here smile and relief spreads like sunshine across her face. "Hey," she says, walking toward us, "I sent you a text—"

"Lizzie doesn't text," blurts Jan. Jade glances at Jan, me, back and forth, as Jan adds, "She thinks it degrades language." Jade and I both stare at Jan. "You know, disrespects the power of words. Even her e-mails—she hardly ever abbreviates."

I want to say that's not true; I text, just not as much as everybody else, but my jaw is hanging so low it's in danger of hitting the grass. Jade's face is kind, attentive.

"Lizzie wants to be a writer," Jade says simply. Jan strikes back: "Not 'wants to be.' Is." Jade manages a teeny smile. I want to pull the entire lawn over my head. "Yes, she is," Jade agrees. "Jade, this is Jan," I say, thinking, *who I'm so glad is here to give you this warm welcome.* They give each other the world's briefest handshake, then look away.

"I can't stay," Jade says to me. She hands me something wrapped, obviously a book.* "I know you said no gifts, but—my father's waiting." "Jade, that's so sweet," I say, giving her a hug. She's tiny, petite, like a ballerina. She makes me feel like Queen Kong, with feet as big as ocean liners; her feet are small and quick as guppies.

"Nice to meet you," Jade says to Jan, and Jan beams a genuine smile. "You, too." Jade squeezes my hand. "You should come back to group . . . bring Jan," she adds quietly. My shoulders tense. Jan's face changes to a that'll-be-a-cold-day-in-hell grin and we watch Jade walk back toward the driveway.

"You talked about me in group?" Jan puts on her sunglasses.

"Not really—you know," I explain, "just that you and Cathy— how the three of us can talk about being adopted because we all three are . . . " Jan is silent. It makes me nuts when I can't see her eyes. I add, "Nothing beyond that, nothing about *you*—"

"Special delivery!" booms Cornelius, holding a paper plate. His big, graceful hand swoops down, delivers Jan's burger, delivers me.

* The gift from Jade: *Somebody's Daughter,* a novel by Helen Myung-Ok Lee, about a seventeen-year-old Korean girl who was adopted as a baby by a couple in the U.S. She decides to go to Korea to study, and then gets interested in where she came from . . . It's *great.*

V. The Dip-Doo

It might be after the third lemonade but definitely just before
dark when East Village steel drums ring from the speakers
hidden in the bushes and Cathy pulls me out of my lawn chair
twirls me like she'd twirl one of her braids which are flying
in all directions and look kinda dangerous with those pinkish-
white beads tied to their ends which I have to keep ducking
to avoid getting braid-slapped but whatever I do must look
like a smooth move 'cause Cathy starts ducking, too, ducking
and then rising and twirling through the grass around everybody
who've made a big circle with the lawn chairs and citronella
candles . . . my hair is loose and flying, too, mostly in my face
though I don't need to see it just feels good to be dancing
crazy . . . We're whirling dervishes! I sing, thinking of the poet Rumi
who whirled for love & poetry . . . This is called the Dip-Doo!
Cathy sings back now to the tune of Dusty Threads and I can smell
those candles mixed with musk of perfume rising from my body
and grass soft under my feet and in the neighbor's yard fireflies
are starting to send their blinking signals like lighthouses of insect
love and now Margo & Cornelius & Toshi & Robert are twirling too
so I dance toward Jan and reach out my hand but she pulls me
down to chair-level so fast I almost fall on top of her she breathes
fire in my ear *What have you been drinking, Lizzie you're drunk*
but I pull back away pretending not to hear trying next to get

Tim Ryan to dance the Dip-Doo he has rhythm he's a better
dancer than Peter I can tell in the few seconds he twirls before
Jan yanks his arm like he's one of those old manual-start
lawnmowers Gram used to have in her garage *We're leaving*
Jan hisses to Tim though I think her snake imitation is meant for
me and so I try to stop swirling but think if I do I'll topple
like a stack of child's blocks yet as Jan pulls Tim across the lawn
toward the driveway & his car I manage to run after them a pretty
crooked dervish run *Please* I say as Jan slams the passenger door
Tim stands outside the driver's door *GET IN* demands Jan but
he looks at me in a way I'll never be able to describe quite right
then he gets in and *JAN!* I yell through her open window I plead
Don't go and she says *Promise me you won't do this again*
and I say *What, do what* and she just shakes her head and won't
look at me *Drink lots of water* is all she says as Tim starts
the car and backs down the driveway and then Cathy
is behind me pulling my arm whirling me back to the dance

VI. The Party's Not Over 'Til It's Over

We draw the circle closer, those
of us still left, light
from all the candles casting shadows
and making circles bright

around our feet. The music has
fallen silent but
no one has the energy
to get up and put

on the radio or
wake up our DJ,
sound asleep on
a big blanket BJ

brought but isn't using—not
now, anyway.
I'm wide awake, thinking
of Jan pulling away;

I'm gulping water by the gallon.
Every party has a pooper,
I remember from second grade,
That's why we invited you.

I cough to stuff down a sob.
Around me my friends chatter
and laugh; I try to, too, though
my heart feels torn & tattered.

For a little while I'd
forgotten all my sadness—
the lemonade had brought on
a kind of forgetfulness.

Now there is that empty space
again, which nothing
can fill. "Hey, Lizzie, look
who's here," says Cathy rising

as Tim Ryan's face emerges
from the dark. He carries a long black
case, wears a guitar slung
on his shoulder—"Hey, I'm back,"

he says, "And I think this party needs
some music!" Then he strolls
over to me. "You
okay, Lizzie?" My heart tolls

like a bell. "Yeah, live
music!" says Margo, clapping
as Tim pulls up a chair.
"This is a party—no napping!"

says Tim, pointing his chair
toward Peter on BJ's blanket,
then flashing me a grin. Cathy
looks at me. "I should have bet

you he'd come back, with his
guitar." "He plays a mean round
of golf, too," pipes up Gabriel.
I swear, just the sound

of that guitar makes everything
suddenly seem okay—
the emptiness, that blazing ache
up and flies away.

VII. Finale

Tim knows the songs that get people singing—
"One Black Dog" and "Angels of Bread,"
"Moon on the Mountain" and "Keeping the King"—

Now even Peter is up, and BJ & Margo,
Toshi & Robert are dancing. Instead
of singing I'm playing the egg, which "maestro"

Tim pulled out of nowhere
and tossed to me, as if he knew my head
and heart were too full to bear

much else. Then it's Robert who starts it—
throws some change in Tim's guitar case. "Bread
for the band," he says like a hippie. We dig in our pockets

to do the same as Tim strums "Bad War, Good Fight."
It's a good note to end on. I need to head to bed.
We all hug when it's over, and say goodnight.

Journal Entry #2108: The Morning After, 1

My eyes feel like I spent all day yesterday swimming under chlorine water with my lids wide as quarters. There's a big lump under a sheet on Kate's bed—Cathy, snoring softly. The clock on my nightstand reads 10:43. Early!

I spot the gift that Mom gave me, still wrapped, next to my glass of water. It's small; must be a book of poems. I sit up, take a long haul of water, and pick up the present, covered in blue paper sprinkled with gold graduation caps. I unwrap it carefully so I can reuse the paper.

For a moment I forget about my tired eyes and stinky stomach. It *is* a book, with a cover of soft, embroidered fabric, lavender and rose and cornflower blue. The pages are made of rice paper—thin but strong—edged with gold. A saffron ribbon dangles between two pages, a built-in bookmark. It's a blank book, a book to hold special words, a book for poems I've yet to write. I give it a hug. *Thanks, Mom,* I think, and fall back asleep.

Journal Entry #2108.1: The Morning After, 2

I open one eye: it's just past noon. The lump on Kate's bed has retwisted itself to reveal Cathy's right foot and a waterfall of braids gushing down her pillow. There's a soft knock on the door, then Mom is standing in the middle of the room with a tray. Sometimes Dad brought her breakfast in bed, that very tray piled with pancakes, strawberries, mugs of steaming black coffee.

"Have the dead arisen?" Mom teases, then looks a little startled by what she just said, probably because I look kind of startled myself. We both look away.

"Not yet," Cathy's voice squeaks from down under.

Mom sets the tray on Kate's dresser—mine is too full of photos and knickknacks and piles of books. "Tea, juice, and bagels with cream cheese!" Mom announces, her smile looking kind of forced. My stomach does a back flip. Maybe food would help. Mom sits on the edge of my bed, holds out a small, rectangular box wrapped in yellow paper. Yellow, my favorite color.

I sit up. My head's filled with air. *I have lost my brains,* I think. *Better than a wicked headache.*

"Mom, I love the blank book," I say, taking the gift from her outstretched hand. The box is not heavy, not light. "Open it. This is part two of your present," beams Mom, "and don't spare the paper." Cathy emerges from her sheet, rubbing her eyes like a little kid, her braids flailing out in all directions. "You look like Medusa," I say, starting to giggle. I cough, take a deep breath. The air in my head might swirl into a tornado if I'm not careful. "Open that box, or I'll turn you to stone," she answers, sounding like she's under water. I tear the paper, which Mom takes and crumples in her hands.

"Montblanc!" I let out a little scream, enough to cause a gust of wind between my ears. It's a pen—the most beautiful I've ever seen—silver and black, sleek and comfortable in my hand. My initials, "E.A.M.," are engraved in scripted letters near the top.

I hold it up for Cathy to see. "Cool, Lizzie, it's perfect!"

Mom has that look—the one she had after my team won a basketball game—happy, proud, relieved. "For my favorite poet," she says, and I hug her. Four years ago she'd sat in that very spot on my bed while I read a poem that mentioned my birth parents. She ran out the door like her hair was on fire.

Instinctively I touch my throat, feel for my charm necklace. Usually I take it off before bed and put it in a little box on the dresser, but I don't remember doing that last night. I'm moving kind of slow as I get up. Mom gets up, too, and moves a mug of tea to the table next to Cathy. Walking feels more like swimming; I need to act cool with Mom. But then I open the little box, the one carved out of teak.

My heart is flying around my chest like a bat trapped in an attic, mad to escape.

My charm. It's gone.

56

Gone

I must have lost it dancing the Dip-Doo.
Cathy's kneeling in the grass beside me.
"It's a charm and will find its way back
to you," she claims. This calms me only
a little while. *Where? Where? Where?*
she asks the ladybug crawling on her palm.
"Maybe a spell, an incantation," I say, when
Tim's green car chugs up the driveway.
We both stand. "Your luck's changing,"
Cathy whispers. "Hey, Preppie!" she teases—
he's wearing chinos, a black golf shirt,
and a look that would make a dead
flower bloom. "Thought you might need
help cleaning up," he says, though his smile
fades when he gets a good look at me.
"What's wrong?" I've turned into a statue.
Cathy says, "We're glad you're here—"
explains what's up as I drop back
on my knees. The three of us search for
hours, cleaning the yard and basement,
too, while Mom combs the house.
No one wants to say it, so I finally do—
"It's gone. Forget it. Thanks. *It's gone.*"

Looks Like Rain

Cathy's getting ready to cut off
her braids—no more swirling
them around her finger, no more
girl nights together, her braiding
while I read us poems. Short
means easy in Mexico, she says,
her dark eyes filling like quarry
lakes, deep and a little lonely.
Her skin is coffee ice cream;
her chin, dimpled like my Dad's.
Her body is soft like a pillow.
"I'm gonna be lean, though,"
she laughs, "living on beans!"
I put my hand on her arm—
can't imagine her skinny.
"Gimme a hug," she says, "time
to head to the train." Now
we're both teary. "Here we go
again, Cath—" I try to sound
cheery. "It looks like rain."

I Drive Cathy Back to the Train Station

(She says / I say)

You'll find it, don't worry.
>Yeah, okay.

It was nice of Tim—
>Peter helped set up.

Which would you rather? The boy who sets up,
or the boy who helps clean up?
>Peter wants to get back together.

Stun me. Like I didn't know. What did you say?
>Nothing. Yet.

You're going to Syracuse, he's going to Miami—
>I know, I know.

And then there's Tim. He didn't show up yesterday because
he likes picking dirty napkins out of your lawn.
>. . . I know. Got your ticket?

He helped us for hours, looking for it—
>Got your ticket?

Yeah, I might have to run for it.
>Don't worry—we're golden. See that spot up front?
>You think Jan will ever speak to me again?

Lizzie—
>Write me from Mexico.

I'll try. We won't really have access—
>I know. You'll write me real postcards.

Yes. And try not to let that letter, this search thing mess you up
too much.
>I'll read it 400 more times, then get back to you on that.

Go to group. Jade will go with you.
>Maybe. Maybe when I'm on break this winter.

Love you, Girlie. I did have fun.
>Love you, too.

You'll find it. And Jan will come around.
>Okay.

No crying.
>I'm not.

No Apologies

It's not until I hug Cathy goodbye
and wave to her city-bound train
that I let myself think about Jan.
Cathy and I didn't even get a chance
to talk it over, I was so upset
about my lost charm. Two huge losses

at one party are two too many
in this Year of Losses. I know why
Jan was mad—since her mom
fell for that lawyer and moved
out, her dad's spent way too much
time at O'Toole's. Afternoons

on my way to work, I often see
his truck already in the parking lot.
Jan's been taking over lots
of the business, not just answering
the phone and scheduling appointments
but fixing cars, too—she's that good.

So I know I should call her, or e-mail,
but every time I sit down at the computer
I think, Why do I have to apologize?
I'm not her dad. I'm not drinking
all the time, forgetting she's even alive.
So what, I had those spiked lemonades—

it was my graduation party. No one
who drank that night was driving.
We just had fun—dancing, singing.
And for a little while, for a few short
hours, I felt happy again. What's wrong
with that, Jan? What's wrong with that?

Journal Entry #2109: Hello

Thursday about 5:30 the Hello Shop's front door jingles and my mouth opens to call "Hello!" but nothing comes out. *"Hello,"* says Tim, his smile so bright against his brownberry skin I fear I'll be struck blind if I look at him. My face suddenly feels sunburned.

"Hey," I almost whisper, kind of smiling but trying to act cool, pretending I need to check the price of a vase on the shelf behind me. I know I look tired, wish I were hiding back in cards instead of working the register. My hand reaches to my throat. Each time I do that, I remember with new anguish that my charm is gone.

"You didn't find it?" Tim says to my back. I shake my head. The vase costs $55. It's made in Ireland. I pray I don't break it. "Thanks, though," I say, peeking at him over my shoulder. "For trying to help."

He leans on my counter, says, "Jan told me you were here today." At Jan's name, I swing around. His eyes are solar-powered. My face feels like it could turn water into steam. *You're so obvious, McLane,* I think.

"She did some more work on my car," he explains, since my ability to speak full sentences has yet to be proven. "Oh," I manage, turning back to the vase.

"You sell postcards?" His voice is musical. I point to a rack without even turning around.

He picks out two New Hook cards. My hands tremble as I ring them up.

"Nice to see you, Lizzie. Go see Jan, okay?" he says as he sails out the door. I nod, waving goodbye, thinking, *Hello, Tim Ryan. Hello, hello, hello.*

Making Up at Mack's Auto

The air is cool and smells of oil inside
the garage at Mack's Auto. Hoses, tools,
and tires hang like trophies on three sides
of the walls. I saw his truck at O'Toole's
on my way, so know Mr. Mack is not
here. It doesn't take long to spot Jan's boots
sticking out from underneath an old Fiat.
(Make that ancient.) "Hey, Jan," I call. Her boots
freeze. A metal clanging sound stops, too, then
resumes. I give her left boot a gentle
nudge. "I was just on my way to work when
I thought I'd stop by." The blang of metal
hitting metal makes me jump. Out rolls Jan,
her face oil-black. She lifts an arm. I take her hand.

Truce

I have a truce with my sister, Kate. After years
of weirdness around any talk of adoption—
our own, or adoption in general—I am giving it
up. Privately, I'm calling it the Don't Ask, Don't
Ask Policy, but with Kate I don't even mention
the truce at all. Pretty soon she'll figure it out:
Lizzie has finally given up on that, *thank goodness.*
She knows about The Letter, but hasn't asked
to read it. I'll probably never know if thinking about
adoption makes her afraid, or angry, or confused.
I have a hunch maybe it's all three. I did ask, once.

Mom Says I Need to Get Out of the House More

I'm becoming a hermit; I need to get out more,
says Mom. "You can't lie around all day with the door
shut doing whatever it is you're always doing in there,"
she says. "Why don't you go out with your friends, or
visit the library, go for a walk, get your hair

trimmed?" Cathy's at the orphanage in Mexico for
the whole summer, I explain. Cornelius is on tour
with his band. Toshi and Robert just sit and stare
at each other. Most days Deb's at The Pet Store
at the mall (that place depresses me; it's not fair,

those dogs in little cages!), then hangs out there for
hours when she's not working. She'll be more poor
by summer's end than she is now, and doesn't care!
And Margo's working at that camp as a counselor,
somewhere in New Hampshire. Who else is there?

I see busy Jan when I can. "Those girls at the store,
what about them?" Mom asks. They've asked me four
times already, Jackie and Sharon both, to their
house. But they're older. What if they think I'm a bore?
"Go," says Mom. "Get out of your cave, my little bear!"

Needing More Than a Tune-Up

I wish I were a car that just needed a tune-up, a turn
of the wrench, some spark plugs, a fuel pump,
and I'd be good to go. I wish I could pull into Mack's
Auto and drive away feeling fixed, running like
I just stepped off the assembly line. I'm thinking this,
perched on a stool in the garage watching Jan work
her magic on someone's Isuzu—it's my new
routine, to spend an hour here with her before
I head to work myself. Jan says I'm good
for business sitting pretty in the shop, that men go
for my sun-kissed nose and mane of dark curls
tumbling down my back. But I know for a fact
that guys bring their cars here just to watch Jan
work, all lean and toned in her tank top and jeans,
her strong arms slick with grease and butter-blonde
hair, cut shorter than theirs, showing off her fine-
boned face. "Hey, Ace—Earth to Liz," she says,
and I shake off the daze I'm in. "What you gonna do?"
She's asking again about the search—my heart begins
to stutter. August 18 I turn 18. I always said that's when
I'd start looking for real. The Letter's enough right now,
is all I say. Jan looks up from the car. "It's a lot to absorb—"
I start to explain. "*So,*" she asks, "everything's changed?"
The universe changed, I want to say, but say instead,
"I don't know. I gotta go." I slip off the stool; Jan follows
me outside. "Don't be scared," she says, "I've got your
back." She opens my car door, gives me a squeeze
before I slide in. "Your Dad has your back, too," she says.
I don't say a word, but try to smile as I wave goodbye.

The Hug

Tim's sitting on the bench outside the Hello Shop
when I walk out on my break. I spot him, stop
short. "Hello, cards and gifts!" he chirps. I have
to laugh. "Lunch at Gertie's?" he asks. I'm glad
he doesn't pretend his being here is a coincidence—
he knew this is my lunch hour. Gertie's Diner is way
cool, my favorite lunch place in New Hook, but
I brought my lunch to eat later. Right now, I say,
my plan is to take a walk, if he wants to come.
He jumps to his feet and catches up with me—
I want to get out of sight before Sharon and Jackie
see us, or I'll get teased. There's a path behind
the strip mall that leads to the river. We're quiet
until we reach the water. I've never felt so
comfortable just being quiet with a boy, except
with Peter. I speak first, warning him of poison
ivy along the edges of the trail. "You lost more
weight," he says, as if he's known me all my life.
As if he's my brother. We turn onto the River Walk,
stop to watch two sailboats glide north. "I'm not
trying," I answer—the same thing I've said to Mom,
Jan, Jackie, Kate. I know I look good; I love how
clothes fit. But I know, too, I'm at the edge of being
too thin. A few more pounds and I could look like
one of those strung-out supermodels. Pretty bony.
To think I'd ever have such a problem! "I mean,
you look great," Tim says, though he's got the cutest
ripple of worry on his forehead. I want to touch it,
sweep it away with the thatch of hair the breeze
has blown down across it. I want to trace my finger
along the V of his widow's peak. I realize we're just
standing now, staring at each other, as if we're playing
statue and someone shouted Freeze! "You okay?"
We say it at the same time, then laugh a little. I nod
my head, then shake it, No. Actually, I'm not.

Suddenly I feel so tired, like I need to rest from all
the weight grief brings. I know if anyone understands,
it's Tim. He opens his arms like two great wings.
It feels like a nest inside them.

VS.

Peter is a lumberjack, his arms and legs like trees; his shirts,
red and black flannel. He smells like leaves, like fresh cold air
that clings to your clothes when you step inside a warm house.
His hair is the color of straw, but the wind got hold of that
straw and blew it all over the barn. His feet in those brown boots
look like gunboats, dangerous enough to sink a navy fleet.
But his voice is low and sweet, like a gospel singer or Louis
Armstrong. He lives in his own time zone (though he's never late
for parties)—sometimes when we're together, he seems far
away; I feel so alone. But we have middle-school memories,
picnics and bike rides, basketball high-fives and those kids
from Stone Falls who died. He saw me through the time I was
struggling to say who I was, and didn't care that I'm adopted,
even if sometimes I feel like an alien. Even when I wanted
to break up, he was nice about it (then had another girlfriend
pretty fast). Peter's a good guy. We just weren't meant to last.

Tim is like one of those sleek-muscled Greek boys, an original
Olympian, olive skin glistening in the sun. He's khakis, collar shirts;
or fine-cut jeans and a button-down sheen with those tuxedo-
black eyes. He smells like soap and sunshine; his black hair
is straight and fine, the opposite of mine. He walks like a cat—
as sure as that—and his heart is a warm tortilla that wraps itself
around you and fills you up, spicy hot. His hug's a sand trap
you don't want out of. His voice is a map that shows you the way
home, no matter how far you've strayed. He's got this way of being
there just before you knew you needed a hand in yours, an endless
store of shoulder to lean on. He's only 18, but his soul seems older;
I hate clichés, but he seems wise. When we talk, even when we
don't, he seems not only to hear but to *see* me. Just the way
he says "Lizzie" makes me weak at the knees. We haven't
known each other all that long, but I swear we've been friends
for an eternity. Maybe we knew each other in another century.

Another Perfectly Good Dinner Ruined (By Me)

Kate's potato chowder is a hit at the Hidden Door,
the restaurant where she cooks in Alphabet City.
They've added it to the menu, she says, since
regular customers keep requesting it. Kate places
a bowl of her famous soup in front of Mom,
Bob, then me. She can hold two bowls in one
hand, like a waitress. Bob's girlfriend Angela

is off at some conference in Vegas, "So he's able
to grace us with his presence," says Mom, half-
ironic, half jokingly. Speaking of grace, Kate says,
and we all mumble a quick prayer over our food.
Dad's empty chair seems to stare and ask, *That's
it? No extra blessings on Kate and her chowder?
On Mom, who's just starting to paint again?*

No, everyone's slurping soup, munching crackers,
talking about the weather, which is hot. I'm not
really listening; I hear Dad singing, *"Who threw
the overalls in Mrs. Murphy's Chowder? Nobody
spoke, so I shouted all the louder: It's an Irish trick
that's true—"* and I must be humming along because
suddenly everyone's staring at me, spoons suspended

in midair. "What?" I say, as Kate's eyes fill with
tears. Mom touches Kate's arm as Bob gives me his
"You've done it now, Stupid," look. I feel like
throwing my spoon at him, but set it down instead.
"What?—" I look from Bob to Kate to Mom—
"are we supposed to add Dad now to the list
of things this family doesn't like to talk about?

"Where should we put him, before birth fathers, or
after?" Kate stands so fast she spills her soup. "Oh,
man," groans Bob as Kate runs out of the room,
Mom right behind her. I'm strangely calm as I
meet Bob's gaze. I refuse to be sorry, I tell him.
"Okay, Lizzie," he says, wiping up the spill.
"But still, do you *always* have to speak your mind?"

Birth Mother Ghazal

Jan says until we know them, we can't judge our birth mothers.
Who knows what happened when they were new mothers?

If I find my birth mother, I hope we can be friends.
I'll have to tell her: I already have a mother.

"I don't know who gets the prize for best disappearing act,"
says Jan, "my mother or my birth mother."

"I'm glad I found them," says Cathy, "but we don't talk—
they're both totally nuts, my birth father *and* my birth mother."

Bank security question: "What's your mother's maiden name?"
Which one, I wonder—my mother or my birth mother?

The Letter tells me some things, but there's so much more
I want to know, starting way before my birth, mother.

Kate and Bob both want to have kids someday.
Me, I'm not sure I'm cut out to be a mother.

When I was in foster care, you came to my doctor's appointments.
In this way you were my mother before you weren't, birth mother.

There are more than 210 million orphans in the world—
how rich I am to have two fathers, two mothers.

If I find my birth mother, I'll ask her to call me Elizabeth.
What will I call *her?* I can't, won't call her Mother.

Ballad of One Saturday Night

If Jackie & Sharon tell you you're tall—
        tall enough to pass
for twenty-one; if they say
        you're coming with them this

time, this night, not going home
        to sit in your room and read,
not again—it's Saturday,
        and there's a party you need

attend—don't call your mother,
        say you're going out
to the movies, then for pizza
        so you'll be late, home about

midnight. Don't follow Sharon home
        in your car 'cause
that's where the party is,
        in the field behind her house—

don't let Sharon flatter you
        with her offer of shorts & tank top
(you're skinny enough now to borrow)
        then think you're kind of hot.

Don't sashay into that field,
        confident in flip-flops,
take the beer Jackie hands you
        in a red plastic cup.

No, not that—the beer so cold,
        the sun still high,
Jackie bringing you around,
        her friends saying hi

in such a way you know they know
        you're *that* girl, the one
whose father died not long ago
        the one who freaked, came undone

over birthday cards for fathers, who
        needs to chill, hear
some music, maybe even dance,
        have another beer,

and another—don't lose track
        of just how many,
don't let them fill your cup again
        before it's even empty.

Then when the sun is setting
        and the tiki lamps are lit,
don't think the world might like your voice
        even a little bit,

don't sing along to Boston Cure
        and Zelman's "This Is It,"
don't think you're cool and take a drag
        off Philip's cigarette,

(don't let him have your cell phone number
        or your e-mail, either).
Don't send your flip-flops flying, dancing
        as if you have a fever,

don't let Van fill your cup again;
        you've already had too many—
don't follow Philip beyond the lamps
        (he can't be bad, right? Can he?).

Don't let him kiss you, then touch you there
        where you don't want to be touched
then warn him when you suddenly know
        you drank *way* too much,

which gives him time to pull away
        before you puke on his shirt
but you get his shoes before you hear
        him call you a freakin' flirt

which is really meant for Jackie's ears—
        she's there now, holding your head
and telling you everything's going to be all right
        (and "Philip, you're freakin' dead")—

and later, when you're through throwing up
        (your head's a jackhammer, your mouth
tastes like glue), don't tell Jackie you're driving
        home. She and Sharon both

will insist you stay, call Mom,
        say where you are (leave out
the part about the beer), say
        you're sleeping here. She'll have her doubts

but she'll say yes, then Sharon will give you
        her bed. What a friend
she is, and Jackie, too. You swear
        to both: Never, never again . . .

Thank God for Guardian Angels

If I look a little pale,
if all I want to eat is dry
toast, if I just want
to sleep when I get home,

Mom doesn't seem to notice.
She's lying on the couch
staring at the weather
channel. She lifts a hand

for me to squeeze—
Did you have fun? she wants
to know. *Too much,* I think,
bending low to kiss her

on the cheek. It's weird to see
her lying here on a Sunday
morning. Neither of us mentions
church or what I was doing

at Sharon's house last night.
God knows I didn't act so
bright. I had a couple of (drunk)
guardian angels watching over

me. Jackie's angry words keep
echoing in my head: "Philip,
you're freakin' dead." I wonder
how I could have been so

stupid. Storm warning in effect,
Mom says, staring at the screen.
Just what we need, I say—
I'm going back to bed.

No Such Thing as Never Again

It's a hit song on the radio, just out by Boston Cure:
"No such thing as never again," sings Tanya Wilton
in that pure voice of hers. She's talking about love,
but Jackie and Sharon and I are sharing a bottle,
twisting the lyrics, " . . . pound down nine, and I'll
pound down ten." Our laughter's on full throttle
by the time the song ends. I wasn't going to party
again so soon, but they heard Mom was going
to the city to see Kate for a night, so . . . it wouldn't
be right, said Jackie, if I stayed home alone. Besides,
I didn't have to work on Monday, and they just
bought two bottles of Blackstone Merlot . . . "Pound
down nine and I'll pound down ten," we belt out
as Sharon pours another round, each of us
convinced that booze is our friend—"No such thing
as never again, no such thing as never again . . . "

Prince at Gertie's Diner

I order ginger ale, dry toast. Tim orders Special #4,
the Everything Omelet. "Someone's hung over,"
he says with a wink after the waitress leaves.
Who winks for real? Tim does. Adorable Tim.
"You should come to Jackie and Sharon's next party,"
I say. "Sometimes people bring guitars, and this girl

Beth plays fiddle—she's amazing—and there's
always a keg." He hesitates, then says, "I'll bring
something. That'll be cool." He'll *bring* something?
He cooks? Shops?! He's reading my mind. "I don't
drink, really," he says. Crap! I feel stupid. "No biggie,"
I blurt, "They always have soda." "If Dad gets a call—"

(his father is a volunteer fireman)—"I need to watch
George. My brother." A little brother! Adorable!
"How old is George?" I gulp some water. "Twenty,"
he answers, and I nearly choke. Tim says, "George
is autistic. He doesn't speak. Never has. He doesn't
bite his hands so much anymore, but—he needs me.

Us. My Dad and me, and we have a lady, a physical
therapist, she comes to the house three days a week."
For once, I am speechless, but that's okay because
Tim can tell I'm listening, and goes on. "George
has physical disabilities, too. He's in a wheelchair.
He can walk, but not really well. He's getting better."

I nod, finish my water. I feel special to have Tim
tell me all this. "He's a good guy, George—don't think
he's stupid. He's not. He knows what's going on.
He understands. He can't speak, but he signs. This
morning he told me that I have star-shine in my eyes."
Tim looks embarrassed, but I like that he tells me this.

"He's a poet, like you, Lizzie." Tim pours cream
in his coffee. My brain's synapses are still having
trouble firing. Biology class does explain some kinds
of dumbness. "And you don't drink because. . . ?"
I ask, showing off my thickness. "I have a beer
here and there. But I can't be drunk if he needs me,"

Tim explains, shaking a sugar packet. Of *course*
not. I'm pathetic. He's beyond adorable, he's—
"You're a prince!" I say as the waitress sets down
my toast. Tim's face turns tomato red. "You mean
princess, right, hon?" the waitress says, and we
laugh. I order Special #3, the Veggie Omelet.

Cover-Up

Jan's busy running someone's credit card
when I pop in Mack's on my way to work,
so I study a wall poster: How to Change
a Tire. I should know this. "You should
get Triple A," says Jan to me while
handing the guy his key. "My parents—"
I start, then stop, start again—"My *Mom*

has it, I think, so I guess me, too." "Where
were you? Last night?" Jan changes
subjects like she changes a tire—fast.
My mind chugs like an engine, but
I know my stare looks dumb. She tilts
her head, "I called—I thought you might
want to come over." "Last night?" I repeat,

glancing again at the poster as if it has my
answer. "Oh, the movies . . . with Jackie
and Sharon, after work . . . " "What did you
see?" "Stella . . . from the Dennis Lehane
book." "You saw that already." This is
the exact same exchange I thought I'd have
with Mom, but didn't. Still, I'm kind of

prepared. "Yeah," I say. "It's that good."
Then I add one more lie: "I'd better go.
I'll be late." Jan glances at the clock
on the wall behind the register. My engine's
overheated—I feel it in my cheeks. "Don't
want to be late," says Jan, her face a question
mark, a look I can't shake for days.

Freedom

Kate and Bob have so much
freedom—their own cars, own
apartments, and no one asking
where they've been all night or
telling them when to be home.
Not that Mom's been a pain
about that lately, not like
she used to be—and sure
I have Dad's car now, though
I can't bring it freshman year
at Syracuse. That's when my
freedom *really* begins, *college,*
I'm thinking as I pull into
the driveway. That's when
I notice Kate's car. Kate?
Like I conjured her up.
She and Mom are sitting
at the kitchen table when I
walk in. "Hey," I say, giving
her a hug. What are you
doing here? "Homesick," is all
she says, trying to smile.
Her eyes are watery red—so
are Mom's. I feel homesick,
too, for the happy place this
used to be. Kate hands Mom
a tissue. They blow a duet.
I give Kate another squeeze.

Journal Entry #2110: Postcard from Mexico #1

When Cathy's postcard arrived, I felt
so many things at once: thrilled to hear
from her, disappointed I didn't get
a long letter, excited about her adventure,
full of admiration for her volunteer work
at the orphanage, worried because—
well, anything can happen down there
to an American traveling alone,
and she made no mention of coming
back. *The people here are so sweet,*
she wrote; *I feel as if I'm home.*

Skipping Stones at the River Walk, Talking About College

Each stone stands for something we can't wait for—
"Pizza every night," says Tim, skidding a flat gray rock
upriver instead of across. I try to toss a stone the same
way—"No curfew!" I say, but mine hops only once, then
sinks. "Eighteen holes a day, sometimes twice!" Tim flicks
his wrist; the stone skips one, two, three, four times.
"You have that *now*," I protest, hurling a rock too big to
skip. It founders like my heart does when I think of how
I'll miss him. "Yeah, but not on a scholarship," he says
smiling, but I swear he's blushing, too. I drop my stone;
we're hugging again. "I'm proud of you, and I'll bet
your Dad and George are, too." Tim looks at me, says
that I make him feel like his two feet are planted
solid on this earth. That I make him feel protective.
"I know you don't need a bodyguard—don't worry,"
he adds. I want to kiss his maple-syrup skin, those
French-toast lips. I'm thinking this when my stomach
growls like a sick dog. Tim pretends not to hear, but
I bust up, then he does, too. "Lizzie McLane, I'm going
to miss you," he says, then pecks me lightly on the lips.
My knees are wobbly. I kiss him back. I'm starving.

Journal Entry #2111: Jan Asks Why I'm Not Ready to Search

What if I make contact and she wants nothing to do with me?

What if she's married and I'm her Big Secret?

What if she's married with *kids* and I'm her Big Secret?

What if I *do* have other brothers & sisters? And how will Kate & Bob react?

What if I look like *him* instead of her, and she can't bear to look at me?

What if I learn that some horrible disease runs in my family?

What if we have nothing in common?

What if it takes years and years?

What if she doesn't like me?

What if she's nuts?

What if she's homeless?

What if she's dead?

Politics at the Library

I'm standing in line at the library, waiting to check out
The Real Warnings, poems by Rhett Iseman Trull, one
of my new favorite writers. Jan's got her hands shoved
in her pockets so no one makes the mistake of thinking

she's checking out a book. "Listen to this," I elbow
Jan, about to read her one of the poem titles when who
walks up to us but Jade. She says hi kind of shyly,
and I reintroduce her and Jan. They remember each other,

unfortunately. After the normal "How you doing?" none
of us knows what to say; I pray Jade doesn't bring up
the adoption group, but think she instinctively knows
that's Topic #1 to avoid when it comes to Jan Mack.

I wish the woman at the front of the line would stop
arguing about her fine and just *pay* it. "Whatcha got?"
I ask, eyeing the black hardcover book Jade's holding.
Enough, by a guy named Juan Williams. "It's about

racism," she says. "That's cool," I say, but Jan asks,
"Are you a Republican?" *Uh-oh,* I think. *Please don't—*
Jade is unfazed, as always. "Does it matter?" "What
the hell, Jan?" I say. "I hear him on the radio sometimes

and he's definitely a Republican," Jan says, looking
at me, then accusingly at Jade. The woman holding up
the line stomps away, empty-handed, and we all take
a step forward. "I don't know," says Jade, whose phone

is ringing. "NO CELL PHONES IN THE LIBRARY!"
shouts the woman behind the desk. Jade has this
horrified look as she turns away, whispering into
her phone. "Well, that was fun. Thanks for being so

nice, Jan," I say. "That's twice now. What do you have against Jade, anyway?" I'm not sure if Jan's jealous, or afraid I'll start going to group and we'll see each other even less. "Just—look out," she replies.

Journal Entry #2112: Typical Sunday at the Hello Shop

It's 11 a.m. on Sunday and nobody's in the store. I'm glad to be in the blank card section, straightening—I feel a little blank-headed after spending the night at Sharon & Jackie's again. Sharon's on the register, dozing on her feet, and Jackie's at the gift-wrap table, folding boxes we'll need later, when we get busy. When I called Mom on my way here, she reminded me Bob's birthday is coming—we probably will get mobbed with customers, she joked, after church & brunch hours. I was glad to hear her sound cheerful.

"How's your Mom?" Jackie asks when I sit down to help her with boxes. She's doing #4s, which are big enough to wrap a softball, so I do #6's, the next size up. We fold so three sides are put together, then stack one box inside the other. Lids we leave flat, to fold at the last minute, when we're wrapping something for a customer.

"How'd you know I was thinking about her?" I ask Jackie. She says she's psychic. "You should start charging for your talents," I tell her — "Then you won't have to work two jobs." "Right," she says—"Sharon will be thrilled when I tell her I'm quitting Razor Software and hanging out my psychic's sign instead—that'll pay my rent and for her new roof for sure." "If you're good enough," I say, "she can quit her bookkeeping jobs and just work here." "Don't say that too loud," Jackie says—"She'll be placing my first ad in the paper!" When she laughs, her dark chocolate skin glows.

"What's all the jocularity about back there?" Sharon calls from the register. She's not allowed to leave the front desk unless one of us relieves her, which makes her crazy if she thinks she's missing out on something. "Don't worry," says Jackie—"We're trying to figure out how you can retire early." "Oh! I'm not worried about *that!*" Sharon calls back—"We're both retiring when Lizzie writes her bestseller and sets us up with her millions." "Yeah, poetry," I say, "there's a lot of money in that," though I do have hope that someday I'll write a prose novel. Or a memoir. I'm working on nonfiction stuff in my journal. "Oh, I have faith you'll find a way," Sharon replies—"and you'll have to take care of me; we might be related!"

"She does look more like your sister than Kate does," Jackie says. "That's it," I say—"I'm dying these curls blonde. Who knows what trouble I'll get in if people start thinking we're sisters!" *Who knows is right,* I think—*we could be.*

Before Sharon can answer, the front door jingles and two ladies walk in. I turn to get a good look. *"Too old,"* I must have mumbled out loud. "Too old for what?" Jackie asks. "Oh—" I'm surprised she heard me—"Nothing."

How It Is Villanelle

Until I met Jackie & Sharon, I didn't party a lot.
But hey, I like how beer, or wine, or Coke & rum
take me to a place I call The World That Time Forgot.

For a while, I can pretend life is like it was *before* it got
to be a mess. Finally, I loosen up and have some fun.
Jan says drinkers are in denial about life, but I'm not.

We just go out a couple times a week—not a lot,
or we hang at Sharon's house after work is done.
I like a place I call The World That Time Forgot,

and so do Jackie and Sharon—but we've got
jobs, are responsible—it's not like we're bums.
Jan says drinkers are in denial about life, but I'm not.

So what I party with the girls, sleep on Sharon's cot—
I don't drive home like that. I'm not dumb.
I just like a place I call The World That Time Forgot.

But hey, I am writing, after all—not a little, but a *lot*.
Big deal, I like to party. What? Should I be a nun
instead? Jan would say I'm denying life, but I'm not—
I just like to visit The World That Time Forgot.

Letting Go

Mom takes Dad's reading glasses off the table by his favorite chair.
I find them in a drawer, put them out again. Mom moves Dad's
boots from the mud room to a box marked *Goodwill.* Next to it
is a box filled with suits and ties. I pull out the boots, set them back
where they were. In the box, I also find a book, *Favorite Irish Jokes.*
This goes on the shelf in my room. Mom's sweeping Dad from
the house; I'm the elf who keeps sweeping him back in. "Not *Dad*—
we're not getting rid of *Dad* ever," Mom tells me, "but we have to let
go, too, Lizzie," she says one afternoon after spotting me returning
his razor and shaving cream to the medicine cabinet. She holds me
a long time while I cry, *No, no, no, no, no.*

The Thief Revealed One Afternoon at Mack's Auto

"Play a song for us," Jan said. "I know you have your guitar
in the car." "Please, please," I whined. "We haven't heard you
play in forever, since the graduation bash. *Please* play
for Jan and me that oldie song about the diner and the trash."
So out he went and back he came with his guitar in its black case,

which jingled as he set it down. "It's the change we tossed you
at my party," I said, laughing as I thought, *He's so handsome.*
Does he think I'm pretty? I ran my hand across the leather
case, looked up at Tim as I opened it for him, dizzy with happiness.
Reaching down for his guitar, Tim suddenly looked strange—

a half-smile, half-frown spread across his face. Jan and I leaned in
to take a peek as Tim's look changed to alarm. There, taped inside
the lid, hovering above the pennies and dimes was my graduation
photo AND my missing charm. "Lizzie! Really! I had *no* idea,"
said Tim, putting his hand on my arm. His cheeks glowed

like burners on a stove. *"Don't touch me,"* I hissed. Jan looked
pissed, too. "You did a sloppy job with your little momento,"
she said, staring at the case open like a mouth. "Did you forget
it was there?" "No wonder," I said, "you were so hesitant to play."
"No—I haven't played since—believe me—" he tried.

"BELIEVE?" I screamed, "I have no doubt—the proof's right here,
Tim Ryan. You freakin', *lying* thief." "No! *No!* There's been some
mistake!" cried Tim. "Yeah, yeah, right. Get out. Leave now, you
jerk," answered Jan, kicking the case with her black boot. "Get *out.*
And don't forget your guitar, not to mention all your loot."

Journal Entry #2113

Charm: 1) a practice or expression believed to have magic power 2) something worn about the person to ward off evil or ensure good fortune 3) a trait that fascinates, allures, or delights 4) a small ornament worn on a necklace or chain

—*Merriam-Webster's 11th Collegiate Dictionary*

1) As in "abracadabra," just when you thought you'd found a really nice guy, he turns out to be a total loser. Not just a loser, but a liar and a thief.

2) If I hadn't been wearing my charm all spring, what *else* could have gone wrong?

3) Ironic that Tim had my charm, because he already had plenty of charms of his own. No wonder he had me fooled.

4) I bought a super-strong chain. This charm is never coming off again.

Hangover

Can't lift my head can't stand the smell
of my own perfume still lingering
from last night can't turn on my left
side or my right without having to
puke, which I do into a bucket thankful
for whoever invented plastic and for
Mom's being at the dentist and then
the mall. If I had to run down the hall
I'd never make the bathroom in time
and my head might explode. Sharon
told me this was "No-No Number One,
don't *ever* do it," but I call in sick
to work. I feel like a jerk. Mrs. Bernstein
has no sympathy. She's pissed. I knew
this would happen . . . she knows I was out
with Jackie and Sharon last night.
"Sharon was right," I whisper out loud
as I hang up my phone: "If you can't
party with the big girls, best stay home."

Betrayal

It's like slurping down a bowl of scrumptious soup,
then finding out the cook spat in it. Like walking

to the end of a dock, then noticing—just as the rotten
boards are giving way under your feet—that someone

had thrown the Danger sign into the lake. It's like
giving your first poetry reading (one of the biggest

moments in your life) and your best friend forgets
the date, doesn't show up. Or like coming in second

in a poetry contest, only to find out later the first-
place winner is the judge's girlfriend. It's like being

told a party starts at 7 when everyone else knows
it starts at 3; you arrive just as the crowd is leaving.

It's like someone stealing your dog. No, it's worse
than that. It's trusting someone completely, finally

trusting, thinking maybe even that you love him,
then discovering that he stole the one object

you treasure above any other thing in the world.
You trusted him. You loved a thief.

Postcard from Mexico #2

I wish you & Jan could visit, writes Cathy this time.
The mountains are magical, especially at sunrise.
(Cathy is up at sunrise?) *You'd be surprised how fast*
your Spanish would improve—the kids love to teach
you! You'd like the food, too (spicy hot), and seeing
how these people live might do you a lot of good.
Wow, Lizzie, are we blessed. Write when you can!
You told me about Tim and the charm—I want to hear
the rest of the story. I know you two were getting pretty
tight, and something just doesn't sound right . . .

Te quiero mucho,

Cathy

Missing Each Other

I.

I pretend I'm asleep,
though I just slipped into bed.
Mom knocks softly, peeks into my room.
She wants to know where I've been.

Though I just slipped into bed,
it's after curfew, after 2 a.m.
She wants to know where I've been
but seems afraid to ask.

It's after curfew, after 2 a.m.
and I'm still a little drunk.
Mom seems afraid to ask—
or it's just easier not to know.

I'm still a little drunk.
She wants to know where I've been.
It is just easier not to know?
I pretend I'm asleep.

II.

Mom's asleep on the couch again
curled up like a baby with her blanket.
I want to shake her, wake her up—
I want to ask if we could talk.

Curled up like a baby with her blanket
Mom looks so peaceful. I leave her alone.
I want to ask if we could talk—
maybe that's a stupid idea, anyway.

Mom looks so peaceful. I leave her alone.
She seems so far away, even when she's awake.
Maybe it's a stupid idea, anyway—
but there's so much I need to tell her.

She seems so far away, even when she's awake.
I want to shake her, wake her up.
There's so much I want to tell her, but
Mom's asleep on the couch again.

Reunion Fantasy #1111

(Hello Shop)

I spy her in the sympathy cards one
Sunday afternoon. I don't know how she
got in without my seeing her. How come
she's in that section, I wonder—did she
lose someone she loved more than the sun?
Or is she sending a card to an old
friend who lost someone, someone he or she
loved? I can tell from the tall way she holds
herself she's worth checking out, being bold
enough to ask her if she needs help, just
to get a good look. She wears a small gold
cross around her neck; her hair is more rust
than red, curly like mine, and her eyes—?
Blue, blue, bluer than blue. I stare, and sigh.

My Last Party

I don't know how many people were there
by the time I parked along the dirt road
by Sharon's field, but I had to drive
a ways before finding an empty spot.
I don't know who handed me my first
beer, but it seems I had one almost as soon
as my sandals hit the grass. Sharon was laughing
with two cute guys carrying watermelons;
Jackie was lounging in a beach chair while
a bunch of people hauled branches and logs
out of the nearby patch of woods to make
a bonfire. Jackie and Sharon both waved, but
I knew enough people from other parties, so
they didn't come running over—I had a beer

in my hands; already someone was taking care
of me. The Crows were blaring through speakers
set up in the bed of a green pickup truck.
The air smelled of sunscreen and Utica Club,
the beer they brew 150 miles west of here,
near where Sharon went to college and Jackie
grew up. It smelled of something else, too.
The moon would be full that night—
the Ripe Corn Moon—and though it was only
seven, the air smelled of trouble and it tasted
like soon. I don't know how long I talked
basketball with Van, who was at his usual post
at the keg, or who handed me that strawberry
jello shot. Or was it raspberry? I don't know

if I did one of those or three; I don't know when
I started dancing with Carla and Gigi, though
I remember the sun was setting about then,
how the air felt cooler and shadows swept over
their faces like clouds, and we kept spilling

our beers but Van came by with a pitcher
every other song and we'd hold out our cups.
I don't know where Sharon was then, but I saw
Jackie roasting marshmallows, setting them
on fire then blowing them out, pulling the charred
shell off the sticky stick and popping it into
her mouth. I don't know if I felt hungry, but
I don't think I ate any of the veggie burgers
I smelled grilling—at one point Gigi held out

a bag of chips, and I ate one of those. I don't
remember when Carla took a break, but I saw her
sitting on one of those benches near the fire, then
Gigi was talking with Bill or maybe his name was
Bob and Philip was dancing with me though
I don't know when he arrived or if he was invited.
I tried not to act too happy to see him or to look
at him much even if he was tan and I could tell
he'd been working out. He told me I was
beautiful and I think I pretended not to hear—
what do you say when someone says that,
anyway—instead I think I asked if Jackie knew
he was there, and he told me I have great legs
and I think I blushed in spite of myself. Maybe

he thought it was the dancing and the beer and
maybe it was too dark for him to see. I don't
know when he suggested we walk to the pond—
maybe that's when I said I don't do blonds.
He laughed—I remember that, how handsome
he looked, how harmless, and I remember
he said the moon would be shining on the pond
by then, but I knew it was still too early
for the moon. I wouldn't let him take my hand
as we cut through the path to the pond until

we were beyond the light of the tiki lamps.
The pond was magical—no moon yet, but
the water was still and shining—we were the only
ones there. I don't know if that's when

I took off my sandals, or if I'd done that
dancing, but I started to wade in barefoot
and Philip said I'd wake the fish. That made
me giggle—I couldn't stop giggling, I wouldn't
come out of the water—it was up to my knees—
until he said something about leeches, something
about snakes. I couldn't stop giggling, though,
I remember that and feeling a little dizzy, and
suddenly very drunk, but I don't remember
sitting down or when he started to kiss me.
I don't know if I resisted at first. I don't think
I did. He smelled like coconut sunscreen and
sweat. He tasted like beer. I remember talking
about the full moon in between kisses but thinking

he wasn't listening. I don't know if I tried to stop
him when he put his hand up my blouse or when
he started unbuttoning it—my favorite white
sleeveless blouse—but I don't think I did.
His hands were warm and I wanted them to be
Tim's hands, and then I think I felt a little angry,
like I was with Philip to get back at Tim, because
I remember thinking *Why'd you have to turn out
to be a loser,* then Philip pressed me back onto
the grass. I don't think I moved when he put his
hand on my breast—I still had on my bra, and when
he tried to lift it up I think I stopped his hand, but
then I realized his other hand was unbuttoning,
unzipping my shorts. No, I said. His mouth was

near my ear—he said, Come on. Come on, Lizzie.
No, I said again, No— I'm not sure how many times
I said it, but he didn't stop and had my zipper
down. He was on top of me then, his hand was
sliding into my panties, then trying to push them
down, too. Don't fight it, he said, You want
it, and I felt a kind of rush in my veins, in my
bones, I felt the animal inside me rising wild
with panic and that's when I bit him on the ear.
Hard. I don't know if the blood I tasted was from his
ear or from his shoulder, 'cause I bit that, too,
which made him move enough for me to whip
one knee up and slam him good where it counts.
I don't know how but I managed to get up then—

I could hear him swearing as I ran, zipping up
my shorts as I went, yelping when I stepped
on something sharp but not stopping, running
through warm, humid air then hitting little pockets
of cold—like the old days swimming in Rothenberg's
Pond, I somehow remember thinking that, then
a loneliness for that pond-swimming girl climbed up
my throat and a choke-cry flew out of my mouth—
yet I kept running until I was near the first tiki lamp
at the other end of the path. There, I paused,
buttoned my blouse. I thought I heard him coming
so I ran again along the edge of the light, avoiding
the bonfire and everyone talking, laughing
around the keg until I reached Sharon's house.

A couple were making out near the front door;
they didn't notice when I flew by them

into the foyer. Someone was using the downstairs
bathroom, but I knew where the other one was,
upstairs near Sharon's bedroom. I slipped in,
locked the door. I don't know why I didn't throw
up—I wanted to. Instead, I knelt by the toilet
and cried. I don't know how long I stayed there
like that. When I finally pulled myself to my
feet, I felt calmer. I used Sharon's mouthwash.
I splashed my face, washed my dirty, cut-up
feet, wondered where my sandals were.
Finally, I looked in the mirror. I sucked in my
breath, nearly jumped. Who was that girl staring
at me, blood on her blouse, black under her
swollen eyes? I don't know you, I said out loud.
I don't know you, she said back.

Smart Girl

I'm barely out of my car at Mack's Auto when
Jan is there, at my door. She's dyed her hair blue.
I long to tell her how great she looks, but don't
know what to do—from the scowl on her face
I know I've been wrong, telling myself that calling
from Sharon's place when I was drunk and upset
last night was no big deal. I can't remember exactly
what I said, but I didn't tell her about Philip,
I know that much. *"You,"* Jan snarls, hands on
her slim hips. "I thought *you* were an A student."
I want to curl up and die. She crosses her arms,
stands planted with her boots wide apart like
she's daring me to dart by her, just try.
"What do you mean?" I ask, kind of knowing
already. She throws her words like darts:
"I thought you were smart." My defenses sputter
like a reluctant motor. "I am," I whisper. *"Well—"*
she's practically spitting—"You were dumb enough
to call me from wherever the *hell* you were last
night. Probably Sharon's." She says "Sharon" as if
it's code for *terrorist*. My motor gives out; it's
broken. I can't meet her gaze. "Jan, I screwed up,
it's been so crazy, I didn't mean—I'm so sorry, I—"
"You know," she interrupts as if I haven't spoken,
"ever since you started hanging out with that
Sharon and Jackie you've been this other person.
If you want to be *her*, go ahead. Just leave me alone."
The office phone rings. Jan and I stare at each other,
for how long, I'm not sure. I look away first. Then
she turns, leaves me squirming like a worm on
a hook. The office door slams. I don't just *feel* like
dirt, I *am* dirt. I sit in Mack's parking lot staring out
the windshield until I'm nearly late for work.

But Now

I used to be a daffodil,
    but now I am a brown, dry leaf.

I used to be all of the king's horses,
    but now I'm the egg, cracked open.

I used to be a mountain lake,
    but now I'm a worm.

I used to be Brigid—Irish goddess of poetry—
    but now I'm a pencil snapped in two.

I used to be a blue bird,
    but now I'm a buzzard.

I used to be afraid of monsters,
    but now I am the hole the monster lives in.

I used to be a foundling,
    but now I'm part-orphan, wandering, lost.

I used to be a colorful painting, a seascape—
    but now I'm a tube of paint, all dried up.

I used to be a dictionary, full of words—
    but now I'm a mute.

I used to be a girl worth knowing.
    If you see that girl, tell me where she went.

Forced Confession, Hello Shop

Sharon calls me up to the register—
I figure she needs a bathroom break.
Once I'm behind the counter, she blocks
one side and Jackie appears at the other.
What's up? I ask Sharon, who looks like
a mother. What's going on? I ask Jackie,
who looks like another. "You might call this
our have-a-heart trap," Jackie says.
"We're not moving," says Sharon, "until
you tell us what happened at the party."
My face feels hot. The *party?*... Nothing,
not anything, really, I stammer. "Why
would you lie?" asks Sharon. "Who are you
protecting?" asks Jackie. "Oh, you *guys,*"
I start—but Jackie interrupts. "Lita
and Dave saw you run in the house."
"With blood on your shirt," adds Sharon.
I remember the couple making out—they
saw? "Look," I say, "I'm just gonna take
a break from partying for a while ... it was—
nothing, really ... " "Lizzie, *Lizzie,*" Sharon
comes close, strokes my arm. "We care
about you," Jackie says. *Really?* I think.
She touches my hair, pushes it back
from my face so I can't hide what I've
shoved down all week. That's all it takes—
mascara's running down my cheeks.

Journal Entry #2114

Poems I'm thinking of sending to Mrs. Wohl:

1) "What Metaphors Are For" (She'll like that she stars in it)
2) "Her Again" (Ditto)
3) The poems about Dad's wake & funeral
4) "Needing More than a Tune-Up"
5) "Ballad of One Saturday Night" (What will she think of all the drinking?)
6) "Letting Go"
7) "My Last Party" (Will she call my mother? Call me?)
8) "But Now"

Journal Entry #2114.1

...What if she DOES call Mom? Will she think she has to, knowing I've been partying like I have? Knowing I was almost raped? She might think I'm desperate and ready to jump off a bridge or something.

...If she calls me instead of Mom, she'll tell me *I* have to tell Mom all of this stuff. Or at least show her the poems. As if I don't want to—I do, but am terrified to at the same time.

...What a stupid idea! Maybe I'll just send #1 through #3. When I have time.

...Maybe.

Nightmare

Smell of meadow grass, dusty, warm—
smell of wax & smoke—salt on my
tongue. I weigh a thousand pounds;
something's holding me down. I lie
on my back, unable to move; candles
surround but don't soothe me—
someone's here, circling in the dark.
My heart's a time bomb, echoing
in my mind as the figure slinks from
light to light, blowing the candles out.
I try to scream, but instead just open
my mouth. The only candle left
is the one beside my head. I feel him
close now (I know it's a him), know
he's closing in to blow the candle out,
but still can't move or cry or shout
as he draws near. I hear him say
my name when he gets close enough
to see. There's blood on his cheek,
a crack in his lip. "You asked for it,
Lizzie. You wanted to come here,"
Philip says, as he holds a mirror
just inches from my nose. Now I see
only my face close up, eyes wide
as I watch me slowly disappear.

Prayer

Mom's let it slide
the Sundays I've skipped
church, but today I need
to go, the way a cripple
needs a crutch. *Thank you*
for keeping me safe, I say.
Please—I'm so lost.
Show me the way, I pray.

I swear just these words
bring me a gift: I feel
something heavy inside
begin, very slowly, to lift.

The Sign

It's been raining for days—dark,
dreary weather to match my mood.

But now the rain is beginning
to lighten, the sky's starting

to brighten, and my cell phone
is ringing—it's Peter. Are you home?

he wants to know. Go outside,
he says, your front porch—quick!

Instead I stick my head out
my bedroom window, and there

it is, the sign I've so needed:
not just a single bright band, but

a double rainbow—red, orange,
yellow, green, blue, indigo, violet

shoving out the damp, the cold—
a God-sent show, promising gold.

Journal Entry #2115: The Truth Comes Out

(James Bard State Park)

"I brought a surprise," Peter says as I spread out our old blanket
on a thick patch of grass. Since the rainbow incident, we've been
seeing each other here & there. "What kind of surprise?" I ask,
eyeing the paper bag under his left arm. He's got my picnic basket
in his right hand. "The best," he answers, setting everything
down, opening the bag. He pulls out two wine coolers. "Still cold,"
he beams. My eyes bug out of my head. I feel a sense of dread.

I say, "*Here?* Are you sure? What if a cop comes by?" He twists
both open, hands me one. It *does* look good. I can see Jan, shaking
her head . . . Jan! How I miss her. Two crows land in a nearby tree—
"Go, go, go," they caw. Peter clinks his bottle against mine.
"To freedom," he says, "and the day we're legal." We each take
a slug. Bubbles tickle my throat, my empty stomach burns a little.
I remember how I felt like the undead after the graduation party,

after the parties at Sharon's, especially that last, *the* last one. "Read
me a poem," Peter says, knowing how to bring me back. I read
him "Graduation Party" (leaving out some parts about him).
He says I should be a novelist. (*I am.* He should read my journal!)
He laughs, remembering the Dip-Doo, says he later thought
that's when I lost my charm, spinning around like a nut. He puts
one arm around me, and I feel a pang, thinking of Tim, of that day

I realized he . . . I touch my charm. Peter reaches for another cooler
with his right hand. I open it with my left so we don't have to stop
holding each other. Then Peter looks at my silver basketball
and toasts, "May your charm always hang round that cute little
neck." Clink! Then Peter sings, "You're my brown-eyed girl,"
and I giggle. "How do you know that song?" I ask. He says,
"You know my Mom. The oldies' station." "My Mom, too," I say,

still laughing. Peter looks weird, hurt. "What? Tim Ryan sings it better than me?" I stop. "You're kidding, right?" I ponder how out of the blue that was, pull chips from the basket. Peter says, "I can't believe he had your charm all along." Now I'm looking for salsa. "And how dumb, not taking the thing out of his guitar case. I mean, if you're gonna *steal* something, be smart enough to *hide* it." I stare at Peter. He tears open the chips, pops

one in his mouth. My mind is a five-speed engine, Jan would say—I feel it shift through first gear to second, third, building up to fourth, then—"Peter," I say, steadily. "I never told you *where* I found my charm—only that Tim *had* it." His face turns red as a bull-fighter's cape, and I am suddenly a strong, snorting, murderous bull. "Jan told me," he stammers. "YOU," I say, "are a LIAR." His face reddens more. I'm throwing stuff back

into the basket. "Lizzie," he says, "Lizzie, I just—" "DON'T!" I say, dumping what's left of my bottle into the grass. "It was dumb, a joke that got out of control," he says as I shove him off the blanket. "You were jealous," I say. "You set him up! To make me think *Tim* is an ass, instead of *you!*" Peter hangs his head, looks five years old. "Yeah. Yeah, I did," he answers, then blurts, "But only because I *love* you!"

My five-speed engine hits a brick wall. All of the clanging inside me goes quiet. I want to hug him. I want to kick him in the shins. "Damn it, Peter!" We lock eyes for a second. He tries to touch my shoulder but I swat his arm. Then he bends for the blanket and I whip it out of his hands. He says nothing. I guess there's nothing left to say. Peter stands there, staring at the ground. I grab my basket and stomp away.

Black Mood

Black heart black cloud black
light black mark black swan
black book black coffee black
eye black rot black horse
Black Sea black box black
ice black pepper black crayon
black lipstick black rock black
out black leather black tea
black tie black face black
rose black magic black panther
black power black boots black
gold black Irish black hole
black diamond black belt black
bear black flag black Mass
black lung black market black
powder black sheep black widow
Black Hills Black Sea black
& blue, black & white, black & tan,
black on black, jet black, bone black,
black-eyed Susan black-eyed pea,
in the black, pitch black, back in black,
black humor, onyx, midnight, bruise,
domino, raven, funeral stiff—
tire marks skidding off a road, ending
at the cliff

Hurricane

By the time I get home from work, a storm's brewing
inside my chest. Mom's surprised to see me. "Lizzie!
I thought you were going out with Sharon and Jackie."
"Nope," I say, opening the fridge. The storm's gathering

strength, but I try not to forecast it. *Calm yourself,*
I think, pouring a glass of water. Mom senses something's
in the air, tries to sound cheerful. "How about tomorrow
we go shopping? Did you make your list for college?"

I slam the glass down—Mom jumps. "I'm not going
to college," I almost shout. Mom looks like a gale-force
wind just knocked her down. I'm surprised myself, but
this hurricane has a mind of its own. "What are you *talking*

about?" Mom's got her mad face on, which only whips up
these winds. "I'm-not-going-to-college," I say slowly,
loudly. "Oh, yes you are," challenges Mom, just as loud.
"You can't make me," I say, knowing I sound like I'm ten.

"What do you propose you'll do otherwise, Elizabeth?"
Elizabeth. I'm in deep now. But I feel powerful. Or this
something does. "I'm going to be—a cop. A hairdresser.
Bartender. Travel agent. I'll work for Jan. Join the Peace

Corps. I'll go to Mexico and volunteer at the orphanage
with Cathy." Mom's got her arms folded. She's shaking
her head, making that face that says I'm being ridiculous,
obnoxious. "I'm serious!" I scream. "Watch me!" I fly

to my room, slam the door. I'm a hurricane, raging for
hours, stomping the floor. Ripped photos of Peter can be
measured in inches. By the time my storm passes, it's dark.
The clock says eleven. I fall into bed and sleep, dreamless.

Instead of Going to College

Maybe I'll climb atop a train, make it take me
down the tracks. I'll lie on my back, let rain
wash my face, let sun turn on my freckles
one by three, like lights at dusk. At night
I'll trace stars with my finger, learn the songs
the hobos knew, line by line and bar by bar.

Maybe I'll shinny up an oak and live among
the crows. I'll paint my face black, tie feathers
in my hair, let my nails grow into claws. I'll learn
what the crow knows about the lives of dead things,
lean and caw greetings to my sisters clustered
like wintered leaves on the ground below.

Or I'll live under that ground, dig a room beneath
the grass, make a space amidst roots and worms.
I'll spit in dirt, paste mud on my face. Always chilled,
I'll start to dread the pound of footsteps, the farmer's
till; I'll learn what the moles and mice know about
tunneling a life under earth and snow.

Maybe I'll crawl to the farthest corner of a cave, pull
a bear's hide over my head, draw my knees to my chest.
Drowsy with stone and the heft of air, I'll sleep until
spring, dream of blackberries and engines of bees. The bear
will teach me about time and hunger, then how to find
my way out of there following the scent of sun.

Sorry

I step softly into the kitchen, feeling beat up
and sad. Mom's at the table, drinking coffee
from Dad's cup. She holds it with both hands
and doesn't look up. "I have to work today,"
I almost whisper. Mom is silent as I take my
mug from the shelf. "Twelve to six," I add,
pouring coffee, my new habit. I suddenly
feel sick, though the coffee smells good.
Slumping into a chair next to Mom, I wish
Dad were here, too. Mom's staring out
the window—her face is stone. "I'm sorry,"
I say. She looks at me and nods. "Get ready
for work, Lizzie," she says, gazing back
toward the window. "I need to be alone."

The Broken Place Revisited at 4 a.m.

It's not a cave. It's a room, and the only monster
is me. I am my own fire-breathing dragon. Here,
words sometimes fly from my mouth charred,
unintelligible. But nothing mars these walls—not
even a window or a door—and sometimes the ceiling
and the floor move toward each other, as if they'll
kiss and crush me. The walls are opaque, and it's
hard to breathe. I'm so alone. No one knows I'm here.

Yet, *now* the walls are clear, one-way
glass, and I can see out: there is Mom, taking a nap;
there's Bob, blasting rap on his car radio, kissing
his new girl, Angela; there's Kate on the patio, shouting
something about a groundhog in Mom's shed. And there's
Jan, walking away, shaking her head.

Where's Tim? At the River Walk, pushing
his brother in his chair. Where's Peter? Nowhere to be
found. And Cathy, she's at the orphanage, with nothing
but the sound of children in her ears. Jackie and Sharon
are down at O'Toole's, having a beer.

I don't wish I were there, but now the walls
are fun-house mirrors: my legs look like stilts and my torso
is short and fat; my eyes are too close together, my hair sticks out
this way and that. I can't bear the sight of myself. Who could
love such a rat? Not my birth mother, I'm sure of that.

But maybe *someone* can, as now the walls
form a chapel with windows of stained glass; my body
is sprinkled with hard-candy colors. The room feels
peaceful, like it does at Mass. So I light a candle, whisper
a heartfelt prayer: Let it stay like *this.* Don't let this time be
like all the others. Please, give me a fair chance. Let me create
a place where there's light. And love. And forgiveness.

Peridot Ring

(An early birthday gift from Bob after I call him)

Here is your birthstone, a yellow-green fire.
It symbolizes strength that comes from within.
I hope that it brings you all you desire—
to know you're loved by everyone, kin
by adoption, kin by blood; to know that
you're accepted for who you are, even
if you're a little weird. (You know, too, that
I'm kidding.) This stone will help you strengthen
your other relationships, too—with friends,
with your boss, with boys who think they love you
and those who truly do. It will help you end
connections that aren't so healthy, and do
what you need to get back on the right road.
It won't *solve* problems; it'll lighten your load.

Mom & I Got the Blues

Nothing like a sad song to put a dagger through your heart.
No, nothing like a sad song to beat the crap out of your heart.
So I compile a play list on iTunes, and I call it "art."

Even happy songs now sound lonely.
All those songs Tim sang make me feel so lonely.
I lost him even before he was my one and only.

I make this set of songs, play them over and over.
Songs like little sticks I hit myself with over and over.
Mom comes to my room to complain, then says, Move over.

Mom & I lie on my bed, sharing a box of tissues.
Mom & I slayed by songs, sharing a box of tissues.
Take one look at us, you'd say, Those two got issues.

Finally we start to talk, like we haven't in a while.
Mom & I finally talk—we haven't in a while.
By dinner time, I swear, we've *almost* started to smile.

Journal Entry #2116

Mom wants to see my poems now . . . now that we talked. I'll show her some, probably the ones I almost sent Mrs. Wohl.

She wanted to know Philip's last name, but I wouldn't tell her. It's over and I handled it, I said, and she finally let it go.

I promised her, no more drinking . . . (but didn't add, "until I get to college")!

Postcard from Mexico #3

Lizzie, I've grown so attached to these kids.
There's a girl named Margarita—I call her
"Megita"—she talks a mile a minute, so
sometimes I can't keep up with her Spanish!
She's so smart and affectionate. And Roberto—
I call him "Beto"—will make you laugh while
he breaks your heart. Then there's Pedro, and
Juan (two Juans, actually, 5 and 7), and Maria,
Esperanza . . . I want to bring them all home.
So I might stay for a year—I told Mom & Dad
I might defer school. Dad says I'd be a fool, but
Mom doesn't want to fight me on this if I'm
feeling determined. Now that surprised me!
What do you think is the right thing to do? Write
when you can. I can't believe Peter took the charm,
not Tim! (Well, yes I can.) But nothing's a sure
thing, I guess. Has Jan come around? She will . . .
What did you decide about searching?

Con amor,

Cathy

Intruder at the Cemetery

When I need to talk with Dad, I often
visit his grave. The cemetery's on
New Hook's west side: left on Parker then
right on LaGrange; it's just past the pond.
I adore Dad's bench, because *he* was fond
of the idea—this was the Gemini in him,
Mom says—us sitting at his grave, the pond
making a nice view, and chatting with him.
So today who's there when I arrive? Not Tim
(I wish), but Peter, his head in his hands,
sitting on Dad's bench, saying something to him
I can't hear. Peter was one of Dad's fans,
but who does he think he is? I am *mad*...
Still, who better to spill your heart to than Dad?

What Big Sisters Are For

I pick up the phone quickly, so it doesn't wake Mom.
I almost say, "Hello, cards and gifts!"—but don't.
It's Kate, of course—that time of day. "She doesn't
nap until later," Kate says. "You think I'm making it

up?" I sound snottier than a runny nose, but don't
care. When's the last time Kate called *me,* asked
how *I* am? She's too busy with her life in New York
to think about her little sister. Sure, she works most

nights at that bistro in Alphabet City, but then I'm sure
she and her friends go out clubbing, or hang out
at some cozy bar. She's having fun, forgetting about
New Hook. Who can blame her? I'd like to forget

about this place, too, and most of the people in it.
"Where are you?" Kate asks after a pause. "Kitchen,
sorting mail," I answer, eyeing stacks of catalogs
and unopened envelopes. The air smells faintly

of smoke—last night Mom tried cooking beets
in the microwave, and one burst into flames. It was
the first time either of us had laughed in days—after
we put the beet out. I tell Kate this story, but know

my laugh sounds forced. *Ha ha, Mom and I nearly
burned the house down cooking beets.* Kate's
more awake than I think. "Lizzie, how are *you?*
What's going on?" It's a question I've longed for;

still, it catches me off-guard. "Fine," I say, but
the word sticks like a burr in my throat. *"No,
you're not,"* says Kate, softly. I cough, and that burr
flies out, followed by an avalanche of words.

Kate Says, Come Visit Me in NYC, and One Thing Leads to Another

I.

So much can happen in a few short days.
Mom gives me 100 bucks; Mrs. Bernstein
gives me a Metrocard and three days
off. Next thing I know I'm on the train
headed for Manhattan. It is morning
in Poughkeepsie—all the commuters left
earlier, so I can sit at my window seat staring
at the Hudson with no deafening
ringing of cell phones, people snoring, papers
and lips flapping about the morning news.
From Beacon to Croton-Harmon, Yonkers
to Marble Hill to Harlem, river views
and George Drew's poems help me start to relax.
Then we reach Grand Central, the end of the tracks.

II.

We reach Grand Central, the end of the tracks.
Kate's there to greet me, under the big clock.
We get cheesecake at Junior's, then head back
to her apartment, a forty-minute walk
or a ten-minute cab ride in late morning
traffic. I opt to walk; my pack is light
and I love to watch the people coming & going
as we head east, south, east again, catching sight
of the Chrysler Building right away, then
soon, the Empire State Building to the west.
We talk about all the Christmases when
our family would visit here, the best
places to shop, and everything we'll do
this weekend. *This time,* says Kate, *is for you.*

III.

This weekend, this time, says Kate, *is for you*
as we reach her East Village apartment,
a second-floor walk-up on Avenue
B. We open the door—an assortment
of take-out menus dot the floor. "More for
my collection!" jokes Kate. Ruth, her roommate,
is on Long Island until Sunday or
Monday—I'll have my own room, can sleep late
if I want, says Kate. "Sleep late? Forget that!"
I'm pumped up. "I can't wait to walk East River
Park and Stuyvesant Cove, hear poetry at
the Bowery and at Cornelia Street, over
in Greenwich Village. We'll go to Macy's
and Ess-a-Bagel. It'll be great. You'll see!"

IV.

"Ess-a-Bagel! Poetry! It'll be great, you'll see!"
I tell Kate again as she changes for
work. We have a long, late lunch on Avenue B,
then I drop her off at The Hidden Door,
where she cooks the dinner shift. I head
to hear music in Washington Square Park,
then to Cornelia Street, where Mark Turcotte read
last time I was here. The poems will be dark
tonight, I think, as I head down the stairs,
find a seat. One of my favorite poets—
Laure-Anne Bosselaar—is reading. The air
feels electric, smells like red wine. Now, it's
her! I want to say hello, but I'm too shy.
Then, she reads. I'm sobbing. I don't know why.

V.

Laure-Anne reads. I'm sobbing. I don't know why,
but later I tell Kate how those poems
spoke to me, how they touched something deep inside
me, and I felt something shift. "I'll read them
again," I say, "Maybe then I'll understand."
Kate almost drops her coffee mug. "Why *do*
that to yourself, Lizzie? How can you stand
to go there?" I smile. "Can't you see I need to?"
She stares at me, then her eyes widen. "Come
on," she says, grabbing her bag. "Where?"
I ask, handing her the keys. "We should have done
this ages ago," is all she'll say, care
and conviction on her face as we're on Sixteenth Street, heading
west. Then, there it is: The New York Foundling.

Breakthrough for Kate & Me

(At the New York Foundling)

This is it—where we were born, says Kate.
We gaze up at the place, red brick twelve stories

high, windows framed in light blue. A cross
hangs above the front entrance, flanked

by sculptured reliefs I guess represent the tree
of life, or family trees. Are those the same

thing? It seems welcoming, anyway, inviting
us in, but we don't dare. "All those times

we've come to the city—why didn't we ever
come *here? All* of us, I mean," I wonder

out loud. Kate takes her eyes from the building,
waits for a bus coming up Sixth Avenue

to pass. There is a kind of lightness, a glow
to Kate's face I've never seen before. As if

she's been lugging a heavy box for the longest
time, and finally set it down right here

on the sidewalk. She says, "Mom and Dad used to
visit this place a lot when Bob and I were little."

I stare at the building, afraid if I look at Kate
she'll stop talking. "Every fall, they'd pack us

in the car with a load of pumpkins and apples
and deliver them to the social workers, so they'd

remember us. There were still a few nuns around
from the old days, but I think they were retired.

They'd coo like doves all over Bob and me—and
the goodies, of course—but I don't really remember

details. We never got farther than the lobby. I never
saw any kids." *Foundlings,* I think, *just like us.*

"On the way home, we'd stop for dinner at this place
near West Point." I sneak a peek at Kate, who's

staring at that cross. "That's why we lucked out
and got *you,*" she says, putting her arm around my

shoulder. Now I stare at the cross, afraid I'll cry.
"Mom's already told you—your birth mother had

this list of things, a whole list of what she wanted
for you." I look at Kate, nod. "I don't know what

those things *were* exactly, but I do know our family
fit the description, and those social workers knew

that because they knew Mom and Dad. What kind
of people deliver country pumpkins and apples

to the kids at the Foundling? Margaret and Patrick
McLane, that's who. Good people who love

children. Who love us." Strangers passing by
on the sidewalk don't look twice at two bawling

girls, two young women hugging and hugging
as if they haven't seen each other in years.

Apology to Jan

I hope you'll read this, when you see who it's from.
Kate says hi—I'm just back from the city.
Maybe I'm a city girl, when it's all said and done.

I felt at home there. Kate said I should have come
earlier, instead of wallowing in self-pity.
Jan, I hope you'll read this, when you see who it's from

because I've been thinking, and have a ton
of things to tell you. Kate's been really great—she
thinks I'm a city girl when it's all said and done;

I get around Manhattan so well. Anyway, some
day soon I hope you'll talk to me, forgive me.
I hope you'll read this when you see who it's from—

I've been so lost lately, *and* I've been a bum
for a friend. But my dad didn't raise a bum, did he?
Maybe I'm a city girl when it's all said and done

and that's where I'll end up living, and you'll come
visit. The real me is back, Jan—I don't want to be dumb
anymore. I hope you'll read this, when you see who it's from—
a city girl, when it's all said and done.

Dear Lizzie: An Apology

(Found in our mailbox today)

Please don't be mad at me. It was a stupid thing to do. The charm thing, I mean. After you danced the Dip-Doo at your party, I spotted your silver basketball in the grass. At last, I thought: a chance to be Lizzie's hero—I'll put it around her neck before she knows it's gone. So I slipped it in my pocket, waited for the right moment, but that never came. You were trying to get Tim to dance with you before Jan dragged him away. I was jealous. Then I figured I'd give you back the charm before the night was over, but Tim showed up again and you were all gooey-eyed over him and his guitar. So . . . I didn't plan to tape your picture (you look so sad and beautiful in that photo) and your charm inside his case. But everyone was hugging goodbye—you and Tim *especially*—and it was dark and I just—did it. Quick. Spur of the moment. It was a mean thing to do to you. To Tim. I'll apologize to him, too, but right now I want to tell *you* that I'm sorry. I hope someday you'll see why I did what I did, and forgive me.

I'll always love you.

Peter

Postcard from New Hook

(Picturing the historic stone library)

Lizzie McLane, I heard great news—
at last my name has been cleared!
Please know that I would *never* hurt you.
I can't say the same of Peter, cuz he
screwed things up pretty bad. He e-mailed,
told me what happened, even apologized.
Maybe there's hope for him. Anyway,
I hope *you're* doing okay. If you happen by
the River on Friday, I will happen to be
there, too . . . say, our usual bench . . . noon?
I'll bring lunch. Hope to see you soon!

                    Your friend,

                    Tim

Rendezvous at the River Walk

I.

After five outfits, four different pairs of shoes, and an hour
of fussing with my hair (wondering, is my birth mother's
hair curly? The Letter just says "brown"), I head to the river.
Tim is already there, playing guitar for a young guy
in a wheelchair: George. Tim is singing to him;
he doesn't see me, but I'm near enough to hear,

> *Nothing could be finer*
> *than to be at Gertie's Diner*
> *in the mor-or-or-ning!*
> *Nothing could be sweeter than my Lizzie*
> *when I meet her in the mor-or-or-ning!*

George sees me, lets out a belly laugh. Tim swings
around, turns dark raspberry red, but laughs, too.
He puts down his guitar, stands up, and I walk into
his arms. I didn't know how much I missed his hugs.
I can't believe he's singing a song about *me*. The tune

sounds familiar, maybe something I've heard in a TV
commercial or on the radio. It's a couple of minutes
before I can talk. "I'm sorry," I croak. "Me, too,"
he whispers. "I'm getting your shirt wet," I say.
"I like it like that," he replies.

II.

The three of us are stuffed on cheese, chips, dip,
coleslaw, grapes, and cake. Well, George has eaten
all the cake. He's staring at me as if he's pleased
about something, while Tim tells me about hearing
from Landon, his soon-to-be roommate. George
taps Tim's arm. "Not now," Tim says, then continues

on about how Landon's also a music major and plays
piano, sax, flute, clarinet . . . George slaps Tim's
arm. "Not *now*," Tim repeats, tapping George's arm
just below the elbow. George's hands start to fly
in the air. Tim's hands dip and swoop and tap back.
"I forgot you *sign*," I say, amazed. Tim's face is burned
bronze. He's smiling, but shaking his head. *"No,
George."* Then he explains to me, "It's kind of our own
sign language." George makes an *ahhh!* sound,
his hands still insisting. "What?" I want to know,
"What's he saying?" Tim looks at me, runs his hand
down my arm. I wish he'd do that again. He looks
back at his brother, says shyly, "George likes you."
I want to hug them both. Instead I reach out my hand;
George touches my fingers quickly, then draws back,
starts signing. This time, whatever he's saying seems
even more urgent. Tim shakes his head *No,* his brown
cheeks still glowing. I want to press my cheek to one
of those cheeks. *"Tell* me," I plead. Tim takes my hand
from my lap. "He wants me to say what I think you
already know," Tim says. I try to look puzzled.
When Tim leans toward me, George beings to clap.

German Potato Salad

It's another hot August afternoon—I'm chopping
celery; Mom, onions, while potatoes boil
on the stove. Where's Gram's recipe? I ask.
Mom points to her head. You know it by heart?
There, too, she says. I don't laugh. That's just
great. Just *super*, I say instead. Are all of Gram's
recipes in your head? I ask. Pretty much, Mom
shrugs. So how am I supposed to make all
that stuff when I'm on my own? I want to know.
Like this, she says, You're learning right now.
Little good that'll do me if you die tomorrow,
I say. We put down our knives, stare at each other
across the counter. I can't believe I just said that,
I say, my hands trembling. Mom is calm as she
walks to a drawer near the kitchen window.
She hands me paper and a pen. I can talk
and chop at the same time, she says. You write.

Postcard from Mexico #4

Believe me, I understand why you want to wait
to search. You've had a crazy year so far,
Lizzie, and now you're going off to S.U.! More
huge changes, more new things to get used to ...
wait until a time when your head is more clear.
I'm glad you'll go back to group, though, if only
now & then. Give yourself at least a year, then
consider it again. I wish I were nearer, but am
so relieved you get why I'm staying—it means
a lot that you believe in me. (I wish Dad did.
Mom says he just worries about my safety.
I couldn't feel more safe!) Promise you'll
write from college, & let me know how it goes
with Tim! So what, you're going separate ways ...
that's not forever. And you know what absence
can do: make the heart grow fonder. (That might
go for you & your birth mother, too.)

Te quiero mucho, Lizzie!

Birthday Party

(A few days before August 18)

I didn't want a bash anymore. I wanted to turn eighteen
with my family, a few close friends. Cathy would be
with me in spirit, she wrote. Dad would, too. I almost
invited Sharon and Jackie, but then thought better of it.
In the end, I invited the people I loved best and hoped
they all would come. Mom strung my birthday cards
from one maple tree to another in the backyard—wishes
from Uncle Rob & Aunt Marge, Uncle Sean & Aunt Sue
(whom I barely knew), my favorite teacher Mrs. Wohl
("Send poems!" she said; I vowed I would), and a slew
of friends. When Jan pulled up the driveway, I practically
flew to her car. "You can't do this without me," she said,
ignoring my arm around her. She saw my hanging cards
and added, *"There's* your family tree." Bob and Kate looked
at each other, then me, and nodded. Bob cracked a joke about
my being part monkey, but I let him get away with it because
next up the driveway were Tim and George. "You said
there'd be cake, so he *had* to come," said Tim, wheeling
his brother across the grass. The picnic table almost felt
complete. I tried to ignore the ache inside me; it was like
a strained muscle that never quite healed. Now
and then the look on Mom's face revealed she
felt it, too, as did Kate and Bob, I knew, though they were
better at hiding it. Yet, there were so many reasons to be
happy! And on this day I *wanted* to be. Mom, who read me
so well, put down the potato salad and hugged me from
behind. "Guess who's here," whispered Kate, and we all
turned. "Hey—hey, Peter, " I said, unsure of whether
to go greet him, or what. I got up and met him halfway.
He was shy as a wallflower, handing me a wrapped gift
I could tell was a book. "I can't stay," he said. I hugged
him quick, saying. "That's okay," trying not to look
relieved. He waved hello to everyone, with a nod to Tim,
and was gone. Then part of me wished he'd stayed. *"Now*
we can eat," said Mom as Bob introduced himself to George,

who signed something back. "If you don't want your cake,"
Tim interpreted, he'll gladly take yours." I gazed around
the table of people laughing, and thanked my lucky stars.

Jan Explains Why She Dyed Her Hair Blue

My mother used to play this song
all the time, "Tangled Up in Blue."
It was about a guy who longed
to find this girl—he thought their love was true.
So he drifted from place to place
while inside, he felt bluer than blue.
Now when I picture my mother's face
along comes another feeling, right on cue.
I long for my *other* mother, who vanished without a trace
and left me here with *no* mother, tangled up in blue.

Changing My Mind (Again)

Jan and I lie on our backs, strewn across my bed,
languid as dogs in summer. A fan at our feet blows

my hair back, away from my face. Jan's tight blue
curls stay put. Without gel, her hair is like a short afro.

Why, she wants to know, won't I start searching
now? "Just register your name," she says bluntly.

"If she's already registered, it might all happen
pretty fast. If she's not . . . well, then you know

and not much has changed, except your strategy."
It could all happen pretty fast! She could be *waiting*

for me! The bed seems to rock like a boat caught
by a surprise wave—but the wave's in my head.

Or my stomach. "I want to be on dry ground first,"
I say, and Jan looks at me funny with one blue eye,

eyebrow raised in an arch. "I mean—I'm waiting
for life to feel more—grounded, more stable."

"Maybe finding your birth mother—*you* finding *her*—
you are now able to be the one *in control* for once,

not some adult who makes all your life decisions for you—
and maybe learning your story . . . why she gave you away,

for starters, will *help*," says Jan. I sit up. I'd never thought
of it that way. The envelope containing The Letter

that I've read 246 times since May seems to sit up,
too, seems to stand and wave like a white flag.

Deciding to Register My Name Online: A Birthday Pantoum

She gave me up for a reason
eighteen years, four months ago—
she might not want to be found.
That's something I must consider.

Eighteen years, four months ago
she signed the papers, she let me go—
that's something I must consider
as I fill out this form, before I e-mail it.

She signed the papers, she let me go—
they promised anonymity. No one had to know.
As I fill out this form, before I e-mail it,
I have to wonder: is that what she still wants?

They promised anonymity—no one had to know
she'd given her baby away. Her name would be a secret.
I have to wonder, is that what she still wants
all these years later? To be a secret?

She'd given her baby away. Her name would be a secret
they would tell no one, unless she decided otherwise,
all these years later, that to be a secret,
to never know me, was no longer an option.

They would tell no one, unless she decided otherwise,
unless she filled out a form, registered her name, because
to never know me was no longer an option
she could live with. Maybe she couldn't live with herself

unless she filled out the form, registered her name, because
that's the only way she'd ever find me. There was hope
she could live with. Maybe she couldn't live with herself
if she *didn't* make it possible for me to find her, as

that's the only way she'd ever find *me.* So there is hope,
unless she doesn't want to be found,
unless she makes it impossible for me to find her.
She did give me up for a reason . . .

Breakthrough for Jan (At Gertie's Diner)

I'm telling Jan about Cathy's plan to stay
at the orphanage in Mexico when Jade
arrives, plops down next to me. "Hey,"
she says to Jan. Whatever weirdness
there was between them seems to have
disappeared. Now instead of being

aggressive, Jan just ignores her. "Thanks
for inviting me," Jade says, pulling her
dark hair back, clipping it with a clear
plastic butterfly. "My treat," I say,
"as a thank-you for that book. I loved it.
I'm mailing it to Cathy." Jade wants to pay,

saying it's my birthday, but I insist.
"That was days ago." When I say this,
my stomach does a flip—I'll be heading
to college in just a few days! "When's
your birthday, Jade?" Her body seems
to stiffen, but she raises her chin a little,

as if this were a matter of pride. "Either
July thirteenth or fourteenth," she says.
"I was found wrapped up on a park bench
in Buscan. The people at the orphanage
couldn't tell if I was a newborn, or a day
old. So they told my parents, anyway."

My cheeks feel warm, but I watch Jan's
face transform, as if she's seeing Jade
for the first time. "I *had* been fed,"
Jade adds, as if to ward off judgment
of the mother who could do such a thing.
After reading the book Jade gave me,

I know the chances of her ever finding
her Korean mother, if she decided to
look, are about zero. Suddenly I feel
privileged, lucky that I have a choice—
to search or not—and that I have a solid
chance of finding my mother if I look

hard enough. The waitress comes at just
the right moment—another thirty seconds
and the silence would be too tough.
We place our orders, then Jan says
something out of the blue: "I admire
you, Jade." Jade blushes, shakes

her head while I pick myself up off
the floor. "It's true," Jan continues,
"You're brave. You have this—history,
and yet you don't cave into it, you know?
You *talk* about it, like 'screw you if
you're gonna judge me if I tell you my

story.'" I'm in awe that Jan's in awe.
Jade smiles. "Come to group," she says.
"Both of you." *You go, girl,* I think—
*strike while the proverbial iron is hot,
as Dad would say!* Jan stares at her
water glass, then at me. I look away,

but I'm smiling. "Lizzie, there's one
more week before you head to college—"
Jade starts to say. "Okay," interrupts
Jan. Jade and I stare at her, speechless.
Jan laughs. "You'd think I just told you
that I won a zillion dollars, and I'm

giving it all to you two." Jade reaches
across the table, touches Jan's hand.
"No," Jade says. "This is even better."

(Stone Falls, NY)

First thing Jan does is stare at the walls. Along two of them, hung in neat rows like Wanted posters, are line-drawings of faces: the typical happy face, like the one you'd insert at the end of an e-mail, plus a sad face, mad face, confused face, scared face, horror-stricken face, bland "who cares" face, surprised face—you name the emotion, there's the picture to match.

"Joe—he's the social worker who runs group—he works with little kids, too," Jade tells Jan. "I guess if they can't express how they feel, they just point." Jan crosses her eyes and sticks out her tongue, and we crack up. I haven't seen Jan act silly since elementary school. "That's my 'I'm-crazy-to-be-here' face," she says.

"All the regulars showed up," whispers Jade when we sit down, "except I've never seen *her.*" She points with her eyes toward a woman across the circle from us. She's about Mom's age, maybe a little younger.

Joe welcomes everyone "new and not-so new," but we don't go around introducing ourselves. I see relief on Jan's face when Joe simply asks, "Who wants to start?"

I've been to group maybe five or six times, and Jade a lot more, but neither of us spoke until our third or fourth session. When at the last second Jan almost changed her mind about coming, we told her she could just listen, and she got in my car.

There are a couple of girls our age whom I recognize and seem to know each other, and a couple of guys who are probably in college. Most of the people—seventeen total—are in their twenties and thirties, except that woman across from us. She's got a super sad face on.

The one Jade and I call "Mad Girl" starts. "I am *so angry,*" she says through clenched teeth, then starts in with "they did this" and "they did that ..." I feel sorry for her but suspect she's half nuts. Later I'll explain to Jan that the girl found both of her birth parents—turns out they married each other and have two more kids. Mad Girl was raised by these two totally messed-up adoptive parents who got divorced when she was ten, so when she found her birth parents and a brother and sister and they were this happy, normal family, she blew her cork. Why the freak did they give her away, she's asking, if they were just going to get married afterward?

I've never seen Jan more attentive. I watch her listening to Mad Girl, then to a guy who's just found his birth mother (the "happy face" doesn't come close to describing his). "He's in what they call 'the honeymoon phase,'" whispers Jade. After Happy Guy, there is Frustrated Woman, who's been searching for eight years. Then three young women around our age speak, kind of as a group; they are all thinking about searching, though one of them mainly describes what it's like to be the only adopted kid with four non-adopted siblings. That would be so hard, I thought. And weird.

One guy with a goatee, who was brought up in an open adoption, details how his two mothers drive him crazy—"They talk about me as if I'm not standing right there!" His stories make everyone laugh, though Jan is pretty subdued. I wish her open adoption were one we could laugh about, instead of being such a joke.

Then one girl in her twenties starts to cry, describing how she told her adoptive parents that she wants to search and they totally flipped out. The guy next to her says he hasn't told his parents he's started searching, for fear they'd react the same way. "It's like it's all about loyalty or something," he explains, and I find myself nodding. "Tell them your needing to know where you come from has nothing to do with how much you love them," suggests Joe, "or what good parents they are. That's all you can do." I nod some more.

There's only about ten minutes left when the older woman across the circle blurts, "I gave my baby up for adoption twenty-five years ago today." Everyone freezes, as if she just pulled a gun. Everyone except Joe, who nods, "I'm sorry, Louise." The woman puts her head down to hide her tears. Joe walks over to her with a box of tissues. She looks up at him and says, "I think about my son every day. Every day, I pray he's all right. I pray he's happy." She grabs a tissue and starts to sob really hard then. I think everyone in the room is crying. The guy who just found his birth mother puts his arm around her. She leans her head against his shoulder and is still crying when Joe says, "See you all next week."

We're halfway back to New Hook before any of us can speak. Finally Jan says, "I didn't know they let birth mothers come." We're silent for a while more. "I hope *my* birth mother feels like that," Jade says. Jan and I just nod.

Journal Entry #2118: Imagine

Peter's mother told me once about a famous folk singer from the 1960s, Joni Mitchell. I'd heard her name before; Mom listens to her. Well, Mrs. Woodward said, did I know the song "Little Green"? It's about Joni Mitchell giving up her baby girl for adoption. (I know the song by heart now. It's on an album called *Blue*.) Years later, the girl found her—they were reunited. Mrs. Woodward didn't know what happened after that.

Imagine finding your birth mother and she's a famous singer! Or movie star. Painter. Photographer. T.V. news anchorwoman. Astronaut. Fashion designer. Writer.

Maybe my birth mother is a writer, just not a famous one. Imagine she lives in New York City—Brooklyn—and she's a housewife who writes stories or poems that haven't been published yet. Or she's a struggling playwright who works as an editor for a big publishing house to make a living. Or she writes annual reports and press releases for the electric company or some Wall Street firm. Or she's a journalist for the *New York Times* or public radio.

Maybe she's not a writer but teaches English at a high school. Or she's a college literature professor. Imagine, I walk into my American Lit class at S.U. and there she is! (Maybe I should be going to N.Y.U.—I do have the feeling she's in the city.)

But she could be anything, anyone. Imagine she's a pastry chef, computer programmer, accountant, seamstress, kindergarten teacher, dog groomer, store clerk, meter reader, doctor, plumber, exterminator, architect, cabinet maker, jeweler, refrigerator repairwoman, maid. Imagine me knocking on her door: she opens it, stares in disbelief, then wraps me in her arms—those same arms that held me once, long ago.

I Go to Tim's to Say Goodbye the Day Before He Leaves for College

Tim holds my hand as we walk along his tree-
lined dirt road, one of the prettiest roads
in New Hook. I gaze up at all the leaves
that soon will be turning red and gold. "Got loads
to pack?" I ask, squeezing his hand. Tim shakes
his head, No. *I wish I could go with you,*
I think, when Tim stops walking. "Let me take
your picture." My cheeks go hot. "What would you do
with that?" I laugh, trying to pull him along.
But he won't budge. He pulls my hand to his
lips. "Please?" Those eyes! It doesn't take him long
to pull out a camera. "I'm not—this—
I wish I'd known," I blurt. "Look at the trees
again," he says. "That's the look I'll take with me."

Off to College

"You couldn't jam another pencil in there," Jan says, staring
at my Subaru. Mom's nodding, her hands on her hips.
"If we get stopped—" "We *won't*," I say through my
teeth, rolling my eyes as Mom turns, heads back into
the house. Jan looks amused. "That's the tenth time

she's said that!" I complain. "Just because you can't see
out the back window—" Jan grins. "What are you two
gonna do without each other to drive crazy?" Now I laugh,
knowing I'll be in tears when Mom drops me at my dorm
and drives away. Jan shields her eyes, peers in the side

window. I expect to see her crying when she pulls
back, but instead she just looks sad. "Did you register?"
she asks. I point to the black-eyed Susans in a vase
on the car's front seat. Mom made an arrangement
to celebrate, I tell her. "That's great. Really cool,"

Jan says. I hug her. "I wouldn't be brave enough if not
for you." Jan hugs me back. I want her to visit me soon
but know she'll say she has to work. "Call me if you hear,"
she says with a weak smile. "Yeah, and a thousand times
while I'm waiting!" Mom comes back outside, locking

the front door behind her. "We should have left room for
Jan," Mom says; Jan's smile brightens. "I gotta get back
to the shop," she says, "and you two gotta hit the road.
You've got miles to go before you sleep." Mom looks
at Jan, surprised. "Lizzie'd be lost without her Frost,"

Jan grins. Mom and I slide into the car; I back down
the driveway, say goodbye to Jan with a beep.
In the passenger seat, Mom lets out a sigh. "Oh, darn
it, Lizzie. I wish your father were here." "He is,"
I answer, one hand on the wheel, the other on my charm.

Self-Portrait

I am summer,
        late August heat.

I am daughter
        four times over.

I'm a shadow
        in the corner of the photograph.

I'm the girl on her knees
        in the stained-glass window.

I have spoken with the ghost
        of the girl I might have been.

(She will never grow up. She'll never speak.
        She wants always to be held.)

I am a song, a ballad, my lyrics lost—
        only the fiddle knows my tune.

I'm the baby in the basket
        feeling blue on a doorstep.

(If you hear me cry,
        I want only to be rocked.)

I'm the foundling in the fairy tale
        carried away by a crow.

(The crow named me, only to find
        I owned that name already.)

I arrived in the winter,
      a snake sloughing her skin.

I'm not shy. I keep the last evening star
      locked in my heart.

(My locked heart, where
      I also keep the broken things.)

Before I was lost I was found.
      There's no shaking me now.

I was a tree, but now I'm paper—
      my ink flows like sap.

Someday my poems will blossom,
      and you'll see yourself in their bright mirrors.

Notes

All bands and song titles (except "Tangled Up in Blue" by Bob Dylan and "Little Green" by Joni Mitchell) are invented by the author. If there are any musical groups or songs in the world that share these names, it's pure coincidence.

There is a fiction writer named Dennis Lehane, but he doesn't have a book called *Stella* (at least not yet). Along the same lines, there is a nonfiction writer named Juan Williams who actually does have a book titled *Enough*. Other living poets referred to in this book are Laure-Anne Bosselaar, Mark Turcotte, George Drew, Donald Hall (and the title poem of his book *Without*), Terrance Hayes, and Rhett Iseman Trull.

Forest Jackson, Poet Laureate of the United States, is a fictional name, as is "The Pet Store."

There's also no such dance as the "Dip-Doo," except in this book.

There actually was a store called "The Hello Shop" in Poughkeepsie, New York, but it's closed now. The author worked there for five years, starting when she was sixteen.

Non-identifying information: some adoption agencies will provide non-identifying information directly to adoptees. Interested adoptees should contact their agency and ask about what kinds of services they provide and what kinds of fees they charge (most are free or no more than $50). In New York State, an adoptee has to be eighteen years old in order to request this information. An adoptee's parents, however, are able to obtain non-identifying and medical information from the time the child is legally theirs. This is why Lizzie's parents sign and mail the form requesting non-identifying information on Lizzie's behalf.

Adoption support groups: there are many such groups around the country; many meet in person, some "meet" online. I highly recommend attending such a group, especially if an adoptee is considering searching for birth relatives.

Adoption registries: there are several websites that offer adoption search services. These sites maintain databases of adoptees, birth parents, and birth siblings who register their names and personal details with hope of finding a match. Some are national, some are statewide. The oldest reunion registries (both existed before the Internet) are the International Soundex Reunion Registry (ISRR), which is free; and the Adoptees' Liberty Movement Association (ALMA), which requires a fee before any information is released. For people adopted in New York State, there is also the Adoption and Medical Information Registry, run by the New York State Department of Health. Most sites are free, but watch for fees (some are hidden) if you decide to register. The trick is, in order for there to be a match, both you and the person you're looking for will have to have registered on the same site. And sometimes the "match" turns out to be a mistake. Many sites will also connect you with a paid searcher, which can cost several thousand dollars. I suggest anyone deciding to go that route use only a searcher who can be recommended by someone trusted, and who asks for compensation only after successfully finding blood relatives.

Guide To This Book's Poetics

Throughout this book, Lizzie writes a mix of formal poems and what's known as "free verse." The following is a brief guide for those who might be interested in taking a closer look at some of the forms and devices Lizzie employs—and just as important, at *why* she chooses the forms she does.

First, a note about punctuation in general.
To a poet, punctuation is similar to musical notation. Since the poet can't always be present to read a poem out loud so people can hear how it is supposed to sound, what its rhythms are, she or he uses punctuation as a guide. Every decision about punctuation—whether to use a period, semicolon, comma, dash, line break with end punctuation (and what particular kind of punctuation it is), line break with no end punctuation, stanza break, etc.—is made with care, as it helps to guide the reader in the poem's pacing and how the poem should sound. Punctuation indicates such things as "pause here for just a breath," "pause here for a tiny bit longer than a breath," "read this part a little bit faster," "go slower here," and "this word is important."

BALLADS
"Ballad of One Saturday Night"

Ballads are narrative poems that usually tell a story that ends in disaster. In olden days, ballads were spoken or sung by people who memorized them and passed them along from generation to generation. The rhymes and frequent use of repetition made them easy to remember.

Ballads are composed in quatrains (lines of four). The rhyme scheme is *abcb* or *abab,* each line with four stresses (words or parts of words that, when spoken, get emphasized more than other words/parts of words) or three.

BLUES POEMS
"Mom & I Got the Blues"; funeral poems; "The Broken Place Revisited"

While many formal poetic forms come to us from Europe and Asia, blues poems are American through and through. They are inspired by the musical form known as "the blues," which springs from African musical roots. Blues poems are usually written in a first-person voice. The classic blues form is rhymed tercets, or three-line stanzas with rhyming end words, in which the first line makes a statement that is repeated with a twist or alteration in the second line. The third line then goes on to make an ironic contrast or extension of what's been said in the first two lines. "Mom & I Got the Blues" is a traditional blues poem.

The writer Ralph Ellison said the blues "at once express the agony of life and the possibility of conquering it through sheer toughness of spirit." These poems usually talk about suffering, struggle, and the dark side of romance. They take on life without flinching, often with wit, sarcasm, and humor. Blues poems don't have to follow the traditional form; some are just plain blue in what they have to say. In this way, the funeral poems, "The Broken Place Revisited," and several other poems in the book could be deemed blues poems.

END-STOPPED LINES VS. ENJAMBED LINES
Lines that have a logical pause at their close (usually with a period at the line's end) are end-stopped; lines are enjambed when there is no end punctuation, and so the sense of one line runs over into the following line. Both types of lines are found throughout the book.

One reason a poet might decide to enjamb a line, or not, has to do with pacing. If a line is enjambed, the reader is drawn down to the next line more quickly than if a line is end-stopped. Unconsciously and at lightning speed, the reader wonders what the next word on the next line will be, and so is pulled down to that word. When several lines are enjambed, the reader is pulled down through the poem as though by an invisible hand. Enjambed lines that include stanza breaks slow the pacing down just a touch. In "Another Perfectly Good Dinner Ruined (By Me)," the last word in the third stanza, "suspended," is itself suspended in midair by being placed at the end of the line just before the break. This both slows down the pace of the sentence and embodies the suspension of the spoons.

Another reason for enjambing a line might be to twist the logic or the meaning of a sentence, and/or surprise the reader with a word or phrase that's not expected.

Here is an example of two enjambed lines from "Journal Entry #2103: Irish Funeral Party":

> I am. I don't want to be
> strong. I just want my life
> back . . .

The first line could stand on its own grammatically; it makes sense as a sentence in which "I don't want to be" could almost mean Lizzie would rather not exist (as in "I am, but don't want to be"); but then, in the next line, we learn she doesn't want to be "strong." Enjambing the line in this way layers the meaning of the sentence ("I don't want to be / strong" slides beneath "I don't want to be") and provides a small element of surprise—the line could simply end "I don't want to be," but "strong" comes in to change and finish the thought.

Similarly, "I just want my life" could stand on its own, too, as in "I just want to be left alone" or even "I just want to live." Instead, we learn in the next line that she wants her life back; she feels as if her life as she knew it has been taken from her.

Another example of enjambed lines can be found in "The Hug": about halfway through the poem (line 17), Tim says, "You lost more / weight." In this novel where loss is a theme, the phrase "You lost more" carries connotations the mind can't help but imagine; then the reader discovers Tim is saying she's lost weight, grounding the sentence in something specific.

Six lines later, Lizzie thinks "I'm at the edge of being / too thin." Someone who is sensing (and frightened by) the fragility of life after the sudden death of her father certainly could feel as if she's "at the edge of being" itself. But here, the reader learns she is (or is also) at the edge of being too skinny.

The sonnet "Peridot Ring" starts and ends with pairs of end-stopped lines; all of the lines in between are enjambed. This causes the reader to pause slightly after each end-stopped line, giving them special emphasis. (The dash after "desire" also slows down the poem, but a little less than the periods do; this way the poem is building slowly toward its slightly faster, enjambed rhythm.) The enjambment of the lines between the first couplet and last couplet draws the reader down through the poem and enables the poet to add layers of meaning and a few slight surprises to the poem:

> to know you're loved by everyone, kin
> by adoption, kin by blood; to know that
> you're accepted for you who are, even
> if you're a little weird. (You know, too, that . . .

Think of each line as a unit in and of itself that gains additional meaning when considered with the line before it and the line that follows. "To know you're loved by everyone, kin" contains its own meaning ("kin" could even be a form of address), but then its meaning builds with the next line: "by adoption, kind by blood." "To know that" could refer to knowing one is loved by these kin, but the sentence continues on the next line, and we learn "to know that" refers to being accepted for who you are. See how that line stands on its own as well? ("you're accepted for who you are, even"!) But again the sentence continues, this time with a humorous twist: "if you're a little weird." This line also could hold its own in terms of meaning, though the syntax is a little backward: "if you're a little weird you know, too, that."

When lines are end-stopped, the pacing is slower. How long the reader should pause depends on whether the end-punctuation is a period, semicolon, or question mark—or any of these marks plus a stanza break. There are no set rules about how long a pause should be, but readers instinctively know, for instance, that a period requires a longer pause than a semicolon; a dash is a bit longer than a comma, and so on.

Here is an example of three end-stopped lines from "Apology to Jan":

> I hope you'll read this, when you see who it's from.
> Kate says hi—I'm just back from the city.
> Maybe I'm a city girl, when it's all said and done.

Each line here is a complete sentence that ends with a period. The poem thus starts slowly, even a bit hesitantly, as Lizzie writes an apology she's not sure will be accepted.

This line is from "Her Again":

> "She's quiet," I say. "She stopped painting."

This is the last line in a quatrain, end-stopped with a period, and then followed by a stanza break. This is one of the longest kinds of pauses indicated by punctuation. It works well here because the pause gives extra emphasis to something that has stopped (the mother's painting).

The poem "Without" begins with a long phrase without punctuation (except for apostrophes) that leaves the reader breathless (much in the way the "Dip-Doo" does in "Graduation Party"). There is no punctuation, no indication to stop until the period at the end of the penultimate line, which does the job of reigning in what, to the reader, feels like a galloping horse. The placement of "chair" at the end of that line gives the word special emphasis. This is followed by the simple, short last line: "Empty chair." The world described in the poem seems to end there, feels lost with that chair. (This poem is based on Donald Hall's poem by the same title, in a book also titled *Without.)*

FREE VERSE

"Prologue"; "First Poem Since the World Changed"; parts of "Journal Entry #2103: Irish Funeral Party"; "It's a Long Way to Normal"; "After"; "Skinny"; the "Dip Doo" section of "The Graduation Party"; "Gone"; "Looks Like Rain"; "I Drive Cathy Back to the Train Station"; "Truce"; "Needing More Than a Tune-Up"; "The Hug"; "No Such Thing as Never Again"; "Freedom"; "Skipping Stones at the River Walk, Talking About College"; "Letting Go"; "Hangover"; "Smart Girl"; "Forced Confession, Hello Shop"; "Nightmare"; "Prayer"; "The Broken Place Revisited at 4 a.m."; "Rendezvous at the River Walk"; "German Potato Salad"; "Birthday Party"; and Postcard from Mexico"

Some people think that "free verse" means the poet doesn't have to follow any rules and can create a poem that has no structure. Actually, there's nothing free about free verse. When a poet writes in free verse, the poem begins to impose its own rules, its own structure upon itself. Once the poet sees what that structure is, it's up to him or her to follow it. For example, if the lines of a free-verse poem start organizing themselves in couplets and in lines that are of medium length (say about ten or eleven syllables), the poet will probably want to create the entire poem in couplets with medium-length lines. In other words, many "free verse" poems are written in strict stanzas, though they usually didn't begin that way in their early drafts. In this *Guide,* I've listed the strict-stanza poems separately from the other free-verse poems so as to highlight that element of their structure.

Even though the poet isn't following any prescribed rules when writing free verse, one would hope that the poem has a sense of music and rhythm, and that elements such as syntax, imagery, metaphor, and line breaks work together to create a poem that captures its reader. Most of the free verse poems in the book feature internal rhyme.

"What Metaphors Are For" is an example of a poem written in free verse, even though it's written in strict stanzas. When those first couple of lines made their way onto paper, they seemed to establish the fact that this was to be a poem made of short lines that averaged between seven and nine syllables each. In early drafts there were no stanza breaks, but in reading the poem out loud I knew it needed to slow down a little and so tried to figure out where the first stanza might end and a new stanza begin. It didn't take long to recognize that if I broke after the line that ends "hovering over me," the line itself would embody that hovering. In a similar way, ending the next stanza with the word "stops" also mirrored the stopping. Amazingly, this gave me two stanzas of six lines each. What would happen if the rest of the poem were in stanzas of six lines each? Experimentation revealed that dividing the poem this way continued to help underscore what was happening in the poem emotionally. But there was one problem: I had two extra lines at the end. Luckily, that couplet ending "rush, a waterfall" seemed perfect on its own, with the space between the penultimate stanza and the last making it seem as if that final lines had "fallen."

When I wrote "Needing More Than a Tune-Up," I broke the first line where I did because I liked the idea of the last word being "turn." ("Verse" comes from the Latin word meaning "to turn.") This established a medium length line, and so the lines that followed are also of medium length, averaging between eleven and fifteen syllables. The poem itself is driven by one main metaphor (the "tune-up") and is driven by enjambed lines that feature a number of internal rhymes.

The postcard poems are also free verse, though the average size of a postcard determined their line length and number of lines; they needed to look as if they could be written on the small square of space that a postcard affords.

GHAZAL
"Birth Mother Ghazal"

In the later part of the twentieth century, a poet from Kashmir named Agha Shahid Ali had a great deal to do with introducing American poets to a Persian form called the ghazal. (Modern translations into English of Persian poets like Rumi and Hafiz helped popularize this form as well.) The ghazal is also found in Urdu and the poetry of other south Asian cultures. It is pronounced "guz-ul," with the "g" sound in the beginning sounding sort of like someone getting ready to spit up something gross.

The ghazal is made of a minimum of five couplets. Usually each line is a complete sentence, although American poets have strayed a great deal from this and other traditional rules of the form. ("Birth Mother Ghazal" uses lines that are complete sentences, even when they are emjambed.) The second line of each couplet usually ends with the repetition of one word, or a short refrain of a few words (such as "mother"). In the first couplet, both lines end in this rhyme/refrain so that the ghazal's rhyme scheme is aa ba ca, etc. The last couplet should incorporate the poet's name.

Usually the theme of traditional ghazals is unattainable love, making it the perfect form for a poet like Lizzie when writing about birth mothers.

LIST POEMS
"Without"; "Black Mood"; "Instead of Going to College"

Also called a "catalog poem," this form has been around for a long time. (The Bible's Book of Genesis, for example, can be considered a list poem that traces the lineage of Adam and Eve's children.)

List poems, which basically itemize things or events, can be made of lines of any length, rhymed or unrhymed.

Lists can provide a powerful structure for an idea to develop and build. "Black Mood" is really just a list of nouns and phrases that include or embody the color black and signify a dark mood. The poem ends in a frightening place.

"Without" is a list to be read fairly fast, as it lacks punctuation. This way it builds quickly toward that final, lonely image: the empty chair.

"Instead of Going to College" is a list written in septets of all the crazy things Lizzie thinks about while she's lying around, sad and exhausted and confused, in her room. It employs a great deal of internal rhyme, and though its mood is fairly dark, it ends on a hopeful note.

PANTOUMS
"The Day My Father Died," "Missing Each Other," "Deciding to Register My Name: A Birthday Pantoum"

This is a French form similar to the villanelle. The second and fourth lines of each quatrain repeat as the first and third in the next, and so on. Though the number of possible quatrains is indefinite, the second and fourth lines of the final stanza must repeat the first and third lines of the first stanza—and ideally, the second and fourth lines of the last stanza should appear in reverse order. Notice how circular this form is, with the first line also being the last line. This means that line has to be very powerful, as it drives home what's central to the poem. This is also a reason for employing the pantoum in the first place.

"Missing Each Other" is made of two short pantoums. The form embodies Lizzie and her mother circling each other but not quite connecting.

"Birthday Pantoum" note: I play with lines a bit in this poem (especially in that last quatrain), but as they say, "You have to know the rules in order to break them."

RHYME
There are various approaches to rhyme throughout the book. While not essential to a poem, rhyme makes a poem memorable and accentuates a poem's rhythm. Here are some examples:

alliteration

Repetition or echo of the first sound of several words in a line; e.g. "Thank God for Guardian Angels" ("Storm," "says," "staring," "screen") and "Skipping Stones at the River Walk" ("Lizzie," "lightly," "lips").

end-rhyme

Repetition of sound(s) are found at the end of lines, as in sonnets such as "Making Up at Mac's Auto" and "Peridot Ring"; or as in "Mom Says I Need to Get Out More," which is rhymed *aabab* and "Jan Explains Why She Dyed Her Hair Blue," which is rhymed *ababcbcbcb*.

identical rhyme

The same word is repeated as rhyme, such as in "First Poem Since the World Changed" ("bench") and "Birth Mother Ghazal" ("mother"). "My Last Party" employs this technique with its repetition of "I don't know. . . ."

internal rhyme

Repetition of sounds within lines and stanzas; just a few examples: "Commencement" ("ark" and "dark," "light" and "upright," "stage" and "LaPage"); and in "vs." ("trees" and "leaves," "fleet" and "sweet," "sunshine" and "fine").

near-rhyme

Sounds repeated are very close, but not exact: as in "sits" and "is," "phone" and "home," "whole" and "drove", or "poster" and "answer."

SIMILE / METAPHOR

When unlike ideas/images, or unlikely resemblances are yoked together, they are referred to as similes or metaphors. Similes are easy to spot because they use the words "like" or "as." The book is full of metaphors and similes—starting with "What Metaphors Are For" ("My chest is blasted / with holes") and "Mother's Day Poem," in which a mother's love is compared with "a bright box of crayons" and "a garden of flowers."

SONNETS

"Dad's Wake," "Dad's Funeral," "Haunted by the Foundling Letter,"

"Making Up at Mac's Auto," "Reunion Fantasy #1111," "Peridot Ring," "Intruder at the Cemetery," "Kate Says, come Visit Me . . . ," and "I Go to Tim's to Say Goodbye the Day Before He Leaves for College." Note the poem "Sorry" is sonnetlike, as it has fourteen lines and is driven by internal rhyme.

A form most people are familiar with, the standard sonnet has fourteen lines written in iambic pentameter. There are different kinds of sonnets, such as Spenserian ("Intruder at the Cemetery" and "Reunion Fantasy #1111") and Shakespearean forms ("Dad's Wake," "Dad's Funeral," and "Making Up at Mac's Auto"), which have different rules about stanza breaks and rhyme schemes. The poem "Kate Says, Come Visit Me in NYC and One Thing Leads to Another" is made of five Shakespearean sonnets strung together, in which the last line of the first sonnet becomes the first line of the next sonnet, and so on. This is a truncated version of what's called a "crown" of sonnets. One version of a "crown" features seven sonnets that work in the way described above, but the last line of the seventh sonnet is also the first line of the first sonnet. In the super-duper form, a "heroic crown," there are fifteen interconnected sonnets, with the last one made, in order, of the first lines of poems number one to fourteen.

Lizzie's sonnets are often "sonnetlike" in that they follow the fourteen-line limit and rhyme scheme of sonnets, but they are not always in strict iambic pentameter. The power of the sonnet is in its compression; a sonnet is able to tell a large story using relatively few lines. Its rhyme scheme also makes it easy to memorize.

STRICT STANZAS
These lines of poetry are organized so that they form a pattern, which is repeated throughout the piece. The word "stanza" means "room" in Italian, and so one could think of stanzas as places that have to be big or small enough to "contain" what's inside them. Stanza breaks, or the spaces between stanzas, indicate a small pause (like a *very* short hallway between rooms). Unless working within a strictly dictated form like a sonnet or villanelle, the length of strict stanzas is something a poet has to decide on her or his own, based on desired timing, effects caused by enjambment, how the poet wants the poem to look on the page, what the poem seems

to be doing "on its own," and gut instinct. In other words, many poems featuring strict stanzas are also written in free verse. See the section on "free verse" for more explication.

Here are the poems written in strict stanza forms:

couplets (pairs of lines)
"The Night Before Graduation" (note this poem ends in a tercet, distinguishing it from the rest of poem, as it is set in the morning when Lizzie wakes up); "Commencement" (the pairs echo the way the students process); "Betrayal"; "But Now"; "The Sign"; "Breakthrough for Kate and Me"; "Changing My Mind (Again)"; and "Self-Portrait"

tercets (three-line stanzas)
"Finale" (from "Graduation Party"; note the rhyme scheme of *aba, cbc, dbd, ebe, fbf*); "Mom & I Got the Blues"

quatrains (four-line stanzas)
"Her Again"; "Back to Work"; "The Party's Not Over 'Til It's Over" (which features an *abcb* rhyme scheme, with a few variations); "Ballad of One Saturday Night" (see also *ballad*); "Thank God for Guardian Angels"; "Politics at the Library"; "Hurricane"; and "What Big Sisters Are For"

cinquains (five-line stanzas)
"Mom Says I Need to Get Out of the House More" (note *aabab* rhyme scheme), "The Thief Revealed One Afternoon at Mack's Auto," and "Off to College"

sestets (six-line stanzas)
"What Metaphors Are For," "Cellar Rat" (from "Graduation Party"), "No Apologies," "Prince at Gertie's Diner," "Instead of Going to College," and "Breakthrough for Jan (at Gertie's Diner)"

septets (seven-line stanzas)
"Another Perfectly Good Dinner Ruined (by Me)" and "Cover-Up"

octaves (eight-line stanzas)
Interesting to note there are none in this book

others

"vs." (16-line stanzas) and "My Last Party" (14-line stanzas).

SYLLABIC VERSE

In this form, the determining feature is the number of syllables in a line, as in "The Night Before Graduation," which has ten syllables per line. It's also organized in couplets. As in writing any strict form, writing in syllabics can produce some surprises—the poet will find herself writing lines she never otherwise would have composed.

VILLANELLES

"Mother's Day Poem I Decide Not to Give Mom," "Reunion Fantasy #1003," "How It Is Villanelle," and "Apology to Jan"

This form, like the sestina and pantoum, comes from the French. It is made of five tercets and a quatrain (nineteen lines total). The first and third lines of the first tercet take turns repeating at the end of the tercets that follow, and both lines repeat as the last two lines of the poem. Notice that there are only two rhymes in the poem, determined by the end words of the poem's first two lines.

Villanelles are great for expressing an obsession; Lizzie's "Fantasy" poems certainly fall into this category, as do the later poems in which she worries over losing Jan's friendship.

About the Author

Meg Kearney was born in the borough of Manhattan in New York City, and placed into foster care under the auspices of the New York Foundling. At the age of five months, she was adopted and brought to live in LaGrange, a town located in New York's Hudson Valley. She grew up there with her parents and two older, adopted siblings.

Kearney has published poetry for both adults and young adults, including *The Secret of Me,* an earlier novel in verse about Lizzie McLane. In 2009, *Home By Now,* her second collection of poems for adults, won the PEN New England L. L. Winship Award and was a finalist for the Paterson Poetry Prize and *Foreword* magazine's Book of the Year. Among her other books are *An Unkindness of Ravens* (poetry for adults) and *Trouper the Three-Legged Dog* (a picture book for children). Many poems, and occasionally a story, have appeared in literary periodicals and anthologies.

Kearney is Founding Director of the Solstice Low-Residency Master of Fine Arts in Creative Writing Program at Pine Manor College in Chestnut Hill, Massachusetts. She has been Associate Director of the National Book Foundation, sponsor of the National Book Awards, and has taught poetry at the New School University (New York).

Meg Kearney frequently visits school classrooms nationwide, where she reads her poetry and discusses craft, and is often a speaker at literary and adoption conferences. She lives in New Hampshire. Visit her web site: www.megkearney.com.

Acknowledgments

I know I am not alone in my belief that Karen Braziller of Persea Books is one of the best editors an author can have. Without her encouragement and thoughtful guidance, I would not have attempted to pursue Lizzie McLane's story beyond *The Secret of Me* and therefore would not have learned so much more about Lizzie's quest for self-knowledge and understanding or just how resilient she can be when the going gets rough. So my first thanks go to Karen and to Persea Books.

From the beginning of Lizzie McLane's journey, my agent Elaine Markson has been there as bellwether and champion, and I am grateful to her.

There are many people who have supported me in the writing of *The Girl in the Mirror* and in all of my literary endeavors: Gabriel Parker, Laure-Anne Bosselaar, Deborah Smith Bernstein, Martha Rhodes, Meg Dunn, Cindy Zelman, Bruce Bennett, Jett Whitehead, Donald Hall, George Drew, Steve Huff, Anne-Marie Oomen, Kathi Aguero, Mark Turcotte, Maureen Petro, and Lita and Dave Judge have all given me invaluable feedback and/or encouragement. It was Jacqueline Woodson, Ann Angel, and Norma Fox Mazer who first inspired me to write for young adults, and saw me through my first verse novel. The students and faculty of the Solstice MFA in Creative Writing Program of Pine Manor College (not to leave out my colleague, Tanya Whiton) have also been more encouraging than they know as I delve into the world of YA fiction.

Special thanks go to Wendy Freund of the Adoption Unit at the New York Foundling (my own adoption agency) for her support and advice, and to the Foundling's legal counsel, Joseph Moliterno.

In 2011, I had the opportunity to reunite with my first- and second-grade teachers, Kathryn Farina and Elyse Mansfield. Besides my parents, these were the first adults who instilled in me a love of reading and an enthusiasm for the written word. I will always be grateful to them and to Titusville Elementary School in LaGrange, New York, where my father was principal.

My parents continue to inspire and encourage me, though they are no longer of this world. My love and gratitude to them—and to my siblings (who inspired the characters of Kate and Bob), nieces, and nephews (who inspired yet more characters, including Tim and George)—is boundless.